Moonlight

CELAENA CUICO

Hardcover ISBN: 978-1-965966-04-4

Paperback ISBN: 978-1-965966-03-7

eBook ISBN: 978-1-965966-01-3

Edited by: Veerie Edits & Vilandra Cuico

Cover by: Gigi Covers

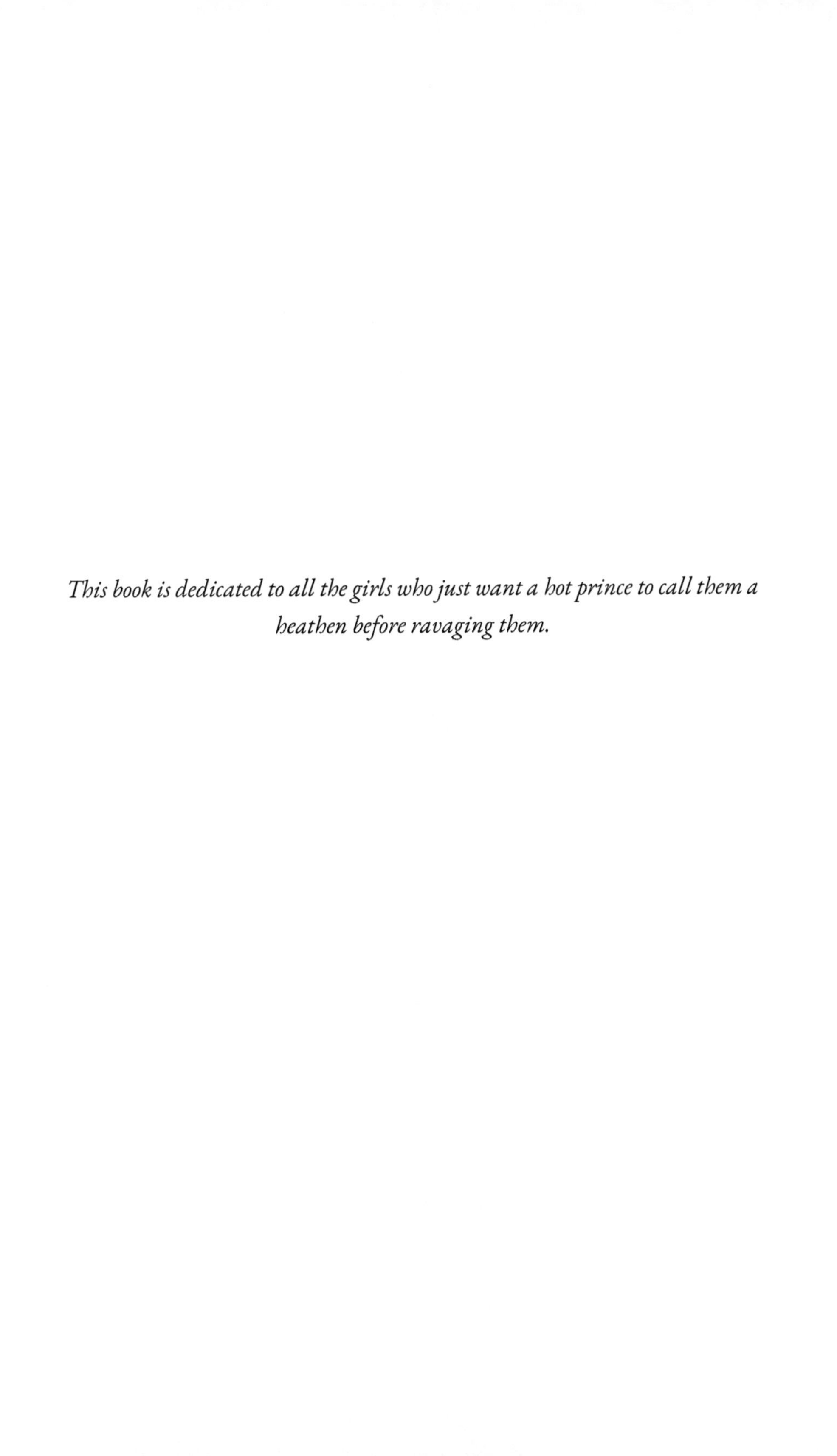

This book is dedicated to all the girls who just want a hot prince to call them a heathen before ravaging them.

<u>The Diadem</u>

Glass and Bone
Cages and Crowns
Moonlight

<u>The Diadem Journals</u>

Elaenor

Tobias

Pronunciation Guide

Characters

Maeryn: May-REN

Evreux: EV-row

Sybil: si-BILL

Amaya: UH-my-uh

Thelonious: THUH-lone-ee-us

Kassius: CASS-ee-us

Demos: day-MOS

Delarus: dill-AR-us

Icana: ick-CAN-uh

Selkath: SELL-kath

Ami: UH-me

Places

Chatis: shuh-TEEZ

Noterra: NO-tare-ruh

Rakushia: RUH-koo-juh

Labisa: luh-BEES-uh

Khailes: KHAL-us

Delaquar Lake: DELLA-car

Brauntie Lake: BRON-tee

Colveil: coal-VEEL

Vaneau: VAN-oh

Tatus: tate-US

Ovobia: OH-vo-BEE-uh

Zivell: ZIV-elle

Aeqerian: ack-KEER-ee-un

Dorin: DOOR-in

Port Tobeo: toe-BAY-o

Senaya Sea: sin-NY-uh

Roally: ROW-uh-LEE

Viridiana: ver-RID-ee-on-uh

RAKUSHIA
CHATIS
DELAQUAR LAKE
ROALLY
RAUNTIE LAKE
VANEAU
RAUNTFORD
NOTERRA
CRAGP
PORT TOBEO
TELLAVID

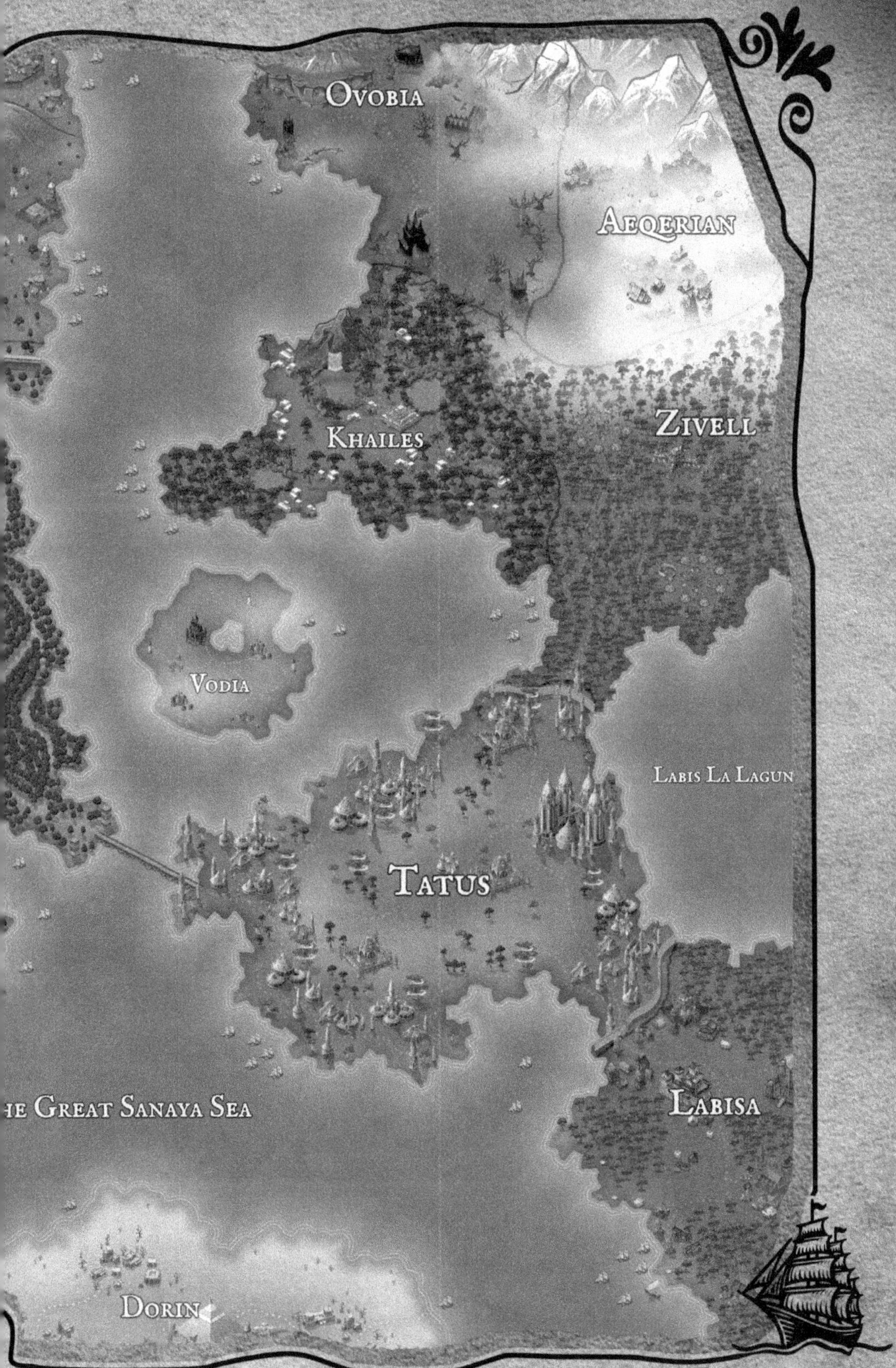

OVOBIA
AEQERIAN
ZIVELL
KHAILES
VODIA
LABIS LA LAGUN
TATUS
THE GREAT SANAYA SEA
LABISA
DORIN

Trigger Warnings

This book is a compilation of my thoughts and experiences. While princesses and magic are something from fairytales, the troubles of women in the modern world are very much real. Suicidal ideation, abusive relationships, sexual assault; those are all things I have experienced in my short life. In a way to prevent myself from succumbing to the ideations of death, I turned the horrors I have faced into a story of perseverance, strength, and the power of finding someone who makes you want to live. But I also threw in magic and fantasy because, why not? I only hope that as you immerse yourself into the world I have created, you find the strength to fight for yourself.

Moonlight includes triggering situations such as graphic violence, gore, murder, graphic language, depression, anxiety, kidnapping, torture, sex, and more.

Prologue

Before there was Elaenor, there was another princess whose story is just as important. The story that starts it all. The war, the bloodshed, the tears, and the battle of crowns.

Resilience.

Revenge.

Tragedy.

Elaenor wasn't the first to experience the pain of royal courts and their games.

The pain of loving a man who ends up breaking her heart.

And she won't be the last.

Part One:

Zivell

Chapter One

The Moon

22 years ago

"Gods, Sybil. Do you have to sneak in here like some sort of ghost?" My mother's irritated voice fills the dark void that is our living area. She's sitting on the couch, reading some form of correspondence like always, and for some reason that only irritates me further. Is it too much to ask for a few minutes of uninterrupted attention?

The living area is large; larger than needed for a family of three. My father spends most of his time in Vodia, where he rules over the waterfolk. When he does show his face in Zivell, he usually comes bearing gifts. Not the kind a daughter would want from their father, but orders and summons and horrible news from the neighboring countries. He never appears simply to spend time with his only daughter.

My eyes scan the large chamber, snagging on the gauzy white curtains pulled back from the open windows. It's raining, like always, and I can feel the heat pouring in. Zivell has a very tropical climate, with humidity, rain, forests, and all types of animals. My mother says it's because our kind need to be close to the earth, close to the Gods. That is why we don't industrialize like other countries. And while I haven't seen these other countries besides Vodia, I can't imagine living in a stuffy palace without the earth beneath my bare feet.

"Sorry, mother," I mutter as I walk around the beige settee and to the banquet table along the wall. Various vegetables and fruits fill the platter, but the pastries are usually my go to for breakfast. I snag a melting chocolate almond croissant and look around again. "Has Kass not awoken yet?"

She's quiet for a second and I take this time to study her. My mother is young, she had me when she was seventeen, making her only thirty-five years of age. She's wearing a white linen dress that flows around her, her feet bare as they rest on the stone. Her hair is a beautiful auburn that looks like fire. She keeps it pinned up into a knot, as do most of us. Heat and humidity have a way of making you hate long hair, but cutting it is also a sign of weakness. The longer your hair, the stronger you are considered.

It's the way of the savages up north, but something we adopted in Zivell as well.

"He already left this morning. He said something about the beach with Ami," she responds after some time. I roll my eyes. My brother has a way of commandeering my only friend when it suits him. I'm not blind, I know they have been lovers since we were fifteen. I warned her not to get too close—our positions usually require arranged marriages—but she disregarded my concern. However, when my brother is forced to marry, she'll come crying to me, and I don't know if that makes me annoyed or secretly...happy.

Happy that I may finally be chosen for once, even if I was the last resort.

I have not had any lovers or relationships of any sort. I flirted, I'm not a total saint, but the idea of entering a relationship held no appeal. My mother has plans, as does my father. I'll marry someone who befits my station, a prince of another country.

So why would I bother getting my emotions and my heart attached to another that I won't be able to keep?

My mother is the Queen of Zivell, although she prefers the term *ruler*. My father is the King of Vodia, making me a princess of two different countries. It was an arranged marriage, hence their comfort in being apart most of the time—actually, *all* of the time. I only wish that I may have a marriage born of love, but I will not be that lucky. Love matches are rare, virtually non-existent, and I have no choice in who I marry. But that thought no longer bothers me.

It's just the way it is.

Amaya is different. She's wealthy and high up in our society, but that is only because her father was on my mother's council before we took her in after their untimely death years ago. Zivell doesn't have Lords or Ladies like most of our neighboring countries. Our hierarchy isn't dependent on wealth or status, it's built upon strength.

My mother goes by the name Firelight, despite her given name of Maeryn. She is a witch, the strongest alive currently. Our bloodline has remained the rulers of Zivell since the beginning of time, and one day, I will take the throne. Zivell is a matriarchal society, so women hold the throne here. My brother will take the throne in Vodia, following in our father's footsteps.

A path that was predetermined for both of us. A path neither of us have the power to change.

I don't think I would if I was able. A life without choice is easy.

Isn't it?

Witches in Zivell are named based on their power. Firelight comes from my mother's inherent aether. Her aether can be used to obliterate, heal, control— pretty much anything. Anything that is her will, the aether can do more or less. Her aether is a bright orangey red, hence the name Firelight. Mine is silver and has earned me the name Moonlight. I am still learning how to wield it, but I can do small magics and create shafts of light that can burn another.

Kassius inherited our father's magics. He's a shifter and a siren. Sirens are the waterfolk and are almost always paired with shifters. All shifters can shift into waterfolk, but not all sirens can shift into other things. Kass is just lucky to be able to do both, as can our father. Our father can shift into nearly anything, but his favorite is what other countries refer to as merfolk. Half human, half fish. It allows him to live below the surface where half of his citizens reside.

Both of us are also Seers. That comes from our mother's bloodline, allowing us to see past, present, and future. While we are too young to be able to control our visions or dreams, in time, we will be able to see nearly anything we want. It's a power I have tried desperately to perfect, but it takes time.

The only vision I have been successful in understanding is the one that happened right before Amaya's parents died. The one that showed me what they took from the earth all those years ago.

The vision that got them killed.

"Will father be visiting soon? He promised to take me with him to Vodia. It has been too long since I have been in the water," I ask as I take a seat across from her. She sighs and sets her paperwork down, her multicolored eyes meeting my blue ones.

"Sybil, no matter how much you try, you will not be able to shift. I know you desperately want to see the underkingdom, but you cannot go below the surface." Her voice is soft, but I know a lecture is coming. It's the same one she always provides and yet I still start this conversation every day.

"Mother, I can hold my breath for nearly five hours now. While I cannot live there permanently, I can still see a small piece of my home."

"Zivell is your home," she retorts.

"It is the only home I have ever known, but half of me will always belong to Vodia." She smiles softly, tilting her head.

"Your brother will be leaving for Vodia on his nineteenth birthday, and you will remain here." She changes the subject, but I knew it was coming. We've been having the same conversation for years.

"Mother, you and father agreed we were better together."

"You will not stay together forever. Eventually your hair will darken, and that needs to happen before you become too attached." Kassius and I have pure silver hair, but we shouldn't. We were born with inky black hair that rivaled the night sky, but as our magics manifested, our hair began to pale.

That's the problem with magical twins. We tend to feed off each other, and the paling of our hair signifies a bond. It means we are connected. If one of us were to die, the other would technically absorb them. My mother has two different eye colors. One of her eyes is a bright hazel that almost glows, the other is an icy blue that is a few shades lighter than my own.

The icy blue belongs to her brother, who was killed when she was a teenager. He was murdered by a rival coven, one who no longer breathes today. She absorbed his magics and she only knew he was gone when she woke up with her auburn hair and multicolored eyes. Death was the only cause for the different eye colors, but distance could change our hair color too.

When Kassius moves to Vodia permanently, our hair will change colors, back to our inky black. There are other causes that could disrupt our hair color, but we only really know of the one connected to our bond or when we are so strong that our magic infiltrates every cell in our body. Being strong enough to channel your aether in your appearance is rare; so rare that I have never seen anyone do it. They would have to have magic on both sides of their family from strong lineages, and while my bloodline is pure and strong, we aren't *that* strong.

But if Kass leaves, I don't know what I would do. My brother and I are close, best friends, and the idea of him leaving for good is terrifying. I can't imagine how alone I will feel. How empty my very body will be without our bond constantly flowing. I reach up and brush my necklace, the feel of it soothing.

"I will be able to visit, will I not?" I pester.

"You will be training, Sybil. You will not have the time nor the luxury of traveling and *vacationing*," She mutters as she reads through her stack of parchment.

"Mother—"

"You are the heir to Zivell. Our legacy is dependent on you. Unless you marry outside our country, you will remain here," she snaps, anger sparking behind her eyes. I nod, averting my own gaze and picking at the croissant.

"Yes, mother." I knew there was no point in arguing with her. She always won. No matter how many times we've had this conversation, nothing ever changes.

"Now, why don't you see if you can catch up to Kass and Amaya. They left not too long ago." Her voice changes into one of pseudo-friendliness. One that she offers to those she's annoyed with but feels as if she should remain pleasant. I nod again and rise from the settee, setting my uneaten croissant back on the table before exiting the room.

The long hallway is bright, lined with torches that glow a bright orangey-red. My mother's aether is what feeds our torches; we never have to worry about them burning out. Every room is cast in the orange glow, aside from mine. A silver glow is ever present in my room. It's one of the only magics I can sustain over time and distance.

I tap the stone pendant hanging from my neck and feel the telltale buzz of aether flowing through my veins.

Where are you? I ask Kassius, my voice echoing through my head as I reach the front door. Armed guards stand on either side of the open door. They are shirtless, with swords strapped along their broad chests and backs. Their long, linen pants are black, and they are barefoot. Not very many people opt for shoes here, something to do with our connection to the earth. Even I, myself, am barefoot. I am wearing a short sundress, a deep blue that reminds me of the ocean.

I can feel the uptick in the buzzing as Kassius responds.

The laguna.

I step out into the humid air and take in my surroundings. We don't have walls here in Zivell, we have our doors open to all. We are completely surrounded by giant trees that take up the same amount of space as our capital palace. White wisps of aether circle around them. That signifies that the rightful heir is sitting on the throne. When the aether dissipates, it means that the person who holds to the title of Queen isn't worthy of it.

I wake up every day hoping that aether goes out, then I would be queen, and my mother would have to step down. *That* would be a sight to behold.

I step out into the grass and make my way to the laguna. Light trickles of rain hit my bare skin and I sigh, relaxing into its comfort. It's still early morning, meaning there are plenty of hours of sunlight left for me to sunbathe, even with the slight drizzle. Kass tans a little easier than I do, something within his siren blood allows that. I envy him, because I was not gifted that particular gene.

His life is a little easier than mine.

My father's kingdom is very...*easy*. Vodia is known for being the island of *savages*. Although less so than the men who live in Ovobia. Those men are the real savages. The people in Vodia are just prone to public indecency and displays of affection, or *carnal need* as my father says. Everyone in Vodia walks around mostly naked and nobody really marries. Everyone co-mingles and accepts all children as the island's children. Nobody wants for anything, as they share any and all resources amongst the citizens. The only one who needs physical heirs is the king, but I am sure I have many half-brothers and sisters on the island or in the underkingdom.

Most of the Vodian citizens are sirens, allowing them to change into merfolk and spend as much time as they want on the bottom of the Senaya Sea. I myself haven't visited the underkingdom in years. Kass can't fully shift yet, but he has mastered his lungs, so he can stay under longer than I can. I can hold my breath for hours, but that isn't due to any siren or shifter abilities, it's just because of my aether. It keeps me alive under most circumstances. The only thing I believe

I truly received from my father is the ability to heal. Water of any kind, as long as it is natural and not a bath, can heal me. If I were to die, my body could be put in the sea, as far out as they can get me within an hour, and if my soul wants to come back, it will.

The water will heal the deep impact of the injuries, leaving only superficial wounds. That is—only if I die from a physical injury. The draining of my aether or some other sickness wouldn't be curable. It doesn't make me immortal; it just makes me a little more resilient than most.

The buzz of aether dies out and I know Kass is otherwise occupied. I nearly gag. Our connection is pretty much always active, unless we are purposefully blocking the other out, which he only really does when he's engaging in *activities,* I would not like to be privy to.

We both have a piece of sirenstone. It's a clear stone that resembles glass that is actually made out of compressed water. It can only be created by a witch, and in our case, our mother made it.

Sirenstone is used to strengthen a preexisting connection, amongst other things. It has to be activated by blood, so when our mother made us our pendants, we had to prick our fingers and spread the blood across the stone. This allows us to have a stronger connection and allows us to draw power from each other. Sirenstone can also help us mindjump, which is what allows us to appear where the other holder of the stone is. We can appear in their head or in front of them as if we were really there.

It's a pretty cool conduit, but it has its limitations. If Kass was drawing from me during a situation in which he is fearing for his life, he can drain too much. It's called siphoning and is illegal amongst our kind. He could effectively kill me or make me mortal, both of which would be abhorrent. Kass isn't a witch, but due to our bond, he could become one if he were to take enough aether.

Siphoning itself is its own magic-form. One my brother could utilize elsewhere and on other people. It's also how Amaya's family took what wasn't theirs.

I steer away from the path to the laguna. There is no way I was about to interrupt whatever the hell my brother and Amaya were doing. I nearly gag again as I take the path to the great tree, relishing in the feel of the warm raindrops landing on my bare skin.

The Great Tree is the largest tree in the country, which is saying a lot since all of the other trees were gigantic. The Great Tree holds the souls of every ruler that has come before my mother. We can seek guidance from the tree and the souls trapped within, or just spend time in their presence.

I often sit under it and work on controlling my moonlight. I feel stronger near them, more in control.

More like a normal girl.

Chapter Two

The Moon

The light dims as I step past the treeline, the silence spreading around me like a thick blanket. But my steps falter as I realize someone made it to the tree before me.

He's tall, roughly six feet or so in height, a few heads taller than me. He has broad shoulders that are straining against the cotton of his tunic, showing a long history of training with weapons, no doubt. Or maybe he's a hand-to-hand kind of guy? He is wearing black trousers that look loose and airy, as if they were made for the humid air of Zivell. His hair is a deep brown, little hints of red shining in the sun reminding me of cinnamon. It's long, tousled waves brushing his shoulders as if it's not used to the climate.

The strange man is facing away from me, his head tilted up to the tree, basking in its size. I stay quiet as I step towards the tree, my aether humming below my skin, wanting to be freed. He doesn't seem like a threat, but I can tell he doesn't belong here.

He isn't *from* here.

And anyone who isn't from here doesn't belong at the tree.

"Who are you?" he asks, and I nearly gasp. There is no way he heard me. His voice is deep, rough, as if he is straining to speak, or that is just the nature of his tone. I find myself wanting to know. My spine tingles and I fight the urge to shudder.

"I should ask that of you, being that you are on my property," I retort, crossing my arms. A deep chuckle reverberates through the air before he sighs and turns towards me.

My mouth nearly drops open at the sight. He has a strong jaw and high cheekbones wrapped in golden tan skin. His eyes are a deep green, almost black, and are framed in thick lashes and bushy brows. They are shaped almost cat-like, with a slight point on the end. His full lips are tilted in a smirk, a shadow of dark stubble covering his jaw. Gods, he's attractive. I force my face to remain neutral as I look away from him, hoping my mask of irritation is believable.

"My apologies, princess." A hint of amusement flickers in his eyes as he bows respectfully.

"I will only ask you this once, Ser, who are you and what are you doing here?" I will my voice to remain steady as I ignore the flutters taking route in my chest. Who is this? And why does he feel so familiar to me? He smiles again, revealing a dimple in his left cheek and two rows of perfectly white teeth.

"My friends call me Archie," he says playfully.

"Well, *Archie*, that only answers one of my questions," I retort.

"My apologies, again, *princess*. I am here as a guest." I cock a brow and suck on my teeth.

"I was unaware my mother had *guests* arriving today," I vaguely respond. He smirks and crosses his arms in front of his chest, mimicking me.

"I am actually here a day early. I remembered visiting this tree when I was younger. I wanted to see it again. You know how a child's imagination is, I found myself questioning if it was real." He turns back towards the tree, his eyes tracking the wisps of aether as they swirl around the emerald leaves. I hesitantly step up next to him, my eyes also following the trails of white. I understand what he means; anyone who did not grow up around the tree wouldn't really believe in its existence. But this was a reality for me.

My nose wrinkles and I make a face as I turn to look up at him. He smells faintly of sea air and...what is *that*?

"Why do you smell like bird poop?" I ask before I can stop myself. He laughs in surprise, the noise echoing off the near silent forest, startling the dozing birds.

"Wow, thank you for your complimentary assessment of my scent, princess," he responds, amused.

"Well?" I press, squeezing my nose to avoid inhaling anymore of the putrid stench.

"I spent the last three days on a very cramped ship filled with supplies and people. My uncle thought I should come bearing gifts to keep your mother as happy as possible," he explains, irritation lacing his voice, but not at me. It seems whatever errand he's on, he's not the biggest fan of.

"And? What gifts have you brought?" I push, curious why he's here. We do get visitors often, but none that look like...*him*. I release my nose and take a step away from him, but it's not the scent that's forcing the distance, it's the pull.

"Chickens, cattle, metal, and jewels. Things your mother most likely has no use of, yet he sent them anyway." Archie's voice trails off in disinterest as he stares in awe. He acts as if he never sees magic, but if he's from the other side of the Senaya, he wouldn't be used to it. They don't have magic over there.

"Explains the salty bird scent," I mutter, and he snorts.

"Maybe you can show me to the closest bathing room so I can make myself more presentable for Your Grace?" He turns towards me, a wicked gleam in his eyes as he bites his bottom lip. I fight the curl in my stomach at the sight. Gods, I hate him already.

"Well, you seem to know your way around here, find one yourself." I spin on my heel, making my way back to the palace as quickly as possible. I have no doubt the man is following me, but I don't look back.

My mother is still sitting in the living area when I barge in, her eyes focused on another piece of parchment.

"Sybil! My Gods," she exclaims as I scare her.

"Mother, are we expecting guests?" I blurt out in a rush.

"Yes, late tomorrow," she says breathlessly.

"Well, they have arrived early," I spit as the sounds of leather hitting stone echoes throughout the room. I turn to see Archie walking in, his hands in his pockets.

"Prince Argent, you are ahead of schedule." My mother smiles as she stands, her voice delighted. Archie drops to a knee, his closed fist over his heart as he acknowledges my mother. *Argent?* As in the heir to Noterra? Rage fills my eyes as I glare at the prince I have quickly come to loathe.

"We hit some good weather across the sea, Your Grace. The winds aided in our travels." He rises and looks over at me, winking. I grit my teeth and face back towards my mother.

"That is wondrous news! I will have you escorted to your chambers so you can rest. Dinner will be served at sundown, and we can discuss in the morning." She turns around, walking back to the couch and motions at one of the guards along the wall. Discuss *what*?

"That would be lovely, Your Grace," he starts. "Actually, your daughter kindly offered to show me to a bathing chamber so I can clean the scent of the sea from me." I narrow my eyes and look over at him. He's biting his lip *again*, holding back a smile as he takes in my expression. Does he ever release it? What is wrong with him?

"Oh, Sybil, how *unusually* helpful of you. You know where to take him," my mother says surprised as she waves us off. Archie – *Argent* – snorts next to me and I glare at him before spinning around and heading down the hallway.

His footsteps are anything but quiet as we trek down the stone corridor, as if he has never had to be stealthy in his life. I'm sure he received some sort of training in combat. If he studied under Abel or Heli, they would murder him on site.

Alright, maybe that is a little dramatic, but they would be displeased.

We pass through the breezeway leading to the other wing of the palace, open walls allowing the cool air to filter through, blowing the humidity away. I take a deep breath as we step back into a closed hallway, cutting us off from the outdoors and the open air.

"You are quieter than I remember," he speaks up from behind me, his deep voice sending shivers down my spine.

"Have we met before? I can't recall," I say nonchalantly as I turn a corner. Double doors are open at the end, revealing the guest wing reserved for esteemed travelers. One of the housemaids is stepping out, an empty basket in her arms as she casts her eyes downwards and hurries past us. I believe that's Daya or her twin Lorna, but I am unsure. Both of them are unusually squirrely.

I hold my arm out. "There." I point towards the room and then turn back down, not waiting for his response.

"That's it?" he sputters, grabbing my hand. He forces me to spin towards him and before I could crash into his chest, I rip myself out of his grasp, stepping back.

"I'm sorry, did you expect me to bathe you?" I snap, my brows furrowing as I stare at this impossible man. His feline eyes narrow and I can tell he's about to say something entirely inappropriate, but I find myself waiting anyway. My arms cross as I stand and my blood heats as his gaze darkens.

"I don't have any of my attendants, so your assistance would be wonderful." He smirks, holding his hand out to me. My jaw drops as I stare at his

calloused fingers, wondering how they would feel around my neck, feel inside—
Sybil. I chastise myself and drop my arms to my side, digging my nails into my palms.

"It wasn't an offer, *prince*. If you seek the touch of a woman, Zivell has some wonderful brothels downtown. Help yourself," I snap before quickly exiting the hallway where we were unsupervised.

Chapter Three

The Fabricated

Her piercing gaze stays at the forefront of my mind, even though I try to shake I off. The water is warm, which I both enjoy and hate. The heat here in Zivell is stifling, and the humidity makes it worse. A bath is almost futile, but at least it'll wash away my apparent stench.

Salt and sea, she said. And bird poop.

She's not wrong. I groan and stick my head underwater, scrubbing my dirty strands. My hair has grown far too long, making it almost unbearable, but I haven't been bothered to cut it.

Maybe I can get the feisty little princess to do it.

No.

I need to stay away from her. Messing around with someone like her can only end in disaster. Common girls were one thing, but princesses had virtues to protect. Although she seems far from innocent to me.

I step out of the bath, water raining down around me, before drying off on a plush towel. For being far-less industrialized than Noterra, they seem to have some luxuries I didn't expect.

I dress in a pair of linen pants laid out for me, a light material to help stave off the heat. Nobody dresses modestly here, and I love it. Tightening the straps around my naked chest to secure my short swords, I step off the patio and into the woods.

Going through the house seemed more like hassle, especially if I ran into the tiny, little heathen.

Gods, how can someone be so annoying and entertaining at the same time? We only spoke a few sentences to one another, but I can't wait to piss her off more.

The moss is soft below my feet, a stark contrast to the rocky woods we have at home. Various shades of pink and white fill the underbrush as their native flower makes itself at home. If I am not mistaken, that sweet floral scent belongs to that of an orchid. A tropical flower I wish we had in Noterra—but we get roses. The most basic of flowers.

I continue, going in no particular direction. It feels nice to be alone in the quiet. I managed to ditch the guards at the port, and I know they aren't even going to attempt to look for me. They will without a doubt be occupying the brothels the next few days we are here. And that doesn't bother me.

It's refreshing not to be followed.

It's more entertaining to follow someone else.

I didn't realize that was what I was doing until I heard her voice. Soft and gentle as she talks to someone. A complete contrast to how she spoke to me.

I peer through the trees at the impossibly white sand, where two females lounge together.

Chapter Four

The Moon

The sand is cool on my feet as I step into the laguna. The rain has stopped, allowing the sun to warm my skin. Ami is lounging topless to the right, Kass nowhere to be seen. I sigh as I walk towards her, collapsing into the relaxing granules of the earth. Ami's skin is glowing in the sunlight, her skin a deep golden olive. The slope of her belly dips down into black swim bottoms, barely covering a single part of her.

"My mother would brand you a whore if she saw you right now." I laugh as I lay back, letting the silver strands of my hair bury themselves in the sand.

"Your mother hasn't seen the laguna in a millennium, I doubt she would choose *now* to come survey this part of her lands," Ami responds, her voice light and carefree.

"Where is my brother?" I ask, noting his absence.

"Under," she sighs, throwing her arm over her face. "He is hellbent on swimming all the way to the underkingdom from here." She sounds resigned, upset.

"It would take days to swim all the way there, even as a fish. He is that eager to leave his home?" I respond, turning my head to look at her. Her blonde hair is tied up in a knot, sweaty tendrils stuck to the side of her face.

"He says Vodia is his home," she whispers.

"He's *wrong*," I snap, hating the venom coating my tongue.

"He says it calls to him, that he can feel it in his bones," Amaya continues, and I almost throw sand at her.

"Tell him to find a mender," I snort. She laughs and turns to face me, curling up on her side.

"One day you both are going to leave me." Her face falls as she reaches forward to cup my cheek, her fingers soft and warm. I turn to curl up on my side, matching her, as I lay my hand over hers.

"I'm not going anywhere, Ami. I promise you." Her gray eyes are saddened, filling with tears. "What is it?"

"I heard one of the members saying that they are working on a deal with some High Lord of Noterra. They said they are planning a marriage alliance for ships." Her voice trails off.

"How did you hear this?" I press. It could just be mere gossip and nothing worth her fear.

"I was acting as the cupbearer at the last meeting, it seems Traya is ill again," she scoffs as she mentions the Hand's daughter. By being sick, she means pregnant. It seems Traya is popping out kids every nine months like clockwork. Her hand slips from mine as she rolls back over. The peaks of her nipples harden as a breeze filters over us, spreading gooseflesh over her skin. I quickly look away, averting my eyes and sighing.

I shouldn't feel this way. I shouldn't *want* this.

But I do.

"Well it couldn't be me. My mother wouldn't marry me off to a lord. She'd reserve me for a prince or a king," I say, keeping the subject political.

"I don't fear it's you, Sy. I fear it's me they are going to sell off." I sit up, raining sand over her face. She spits it out of her mouth and brushes it out of her eyes with a glare. "*Sybil*," she groans in annoyance.

"No. She wouldn't, Amaya," I say sternly, leaning over her. My hair forms a curtain, tickling her breasts and she shivers. She reaches up and grabs my face again, forcing me to stare into her eyes.

"You can't save me from this. It's what I was always made for. Us royals are sold as broodmares to help further a ruler's political reign, you know this. Part of me just always wished your mother would allow Kass and I to marry," she says softly, her thumb brushing my bottom lip.

"Did they say when?" She shakes her head and I groan, resting further into her touch. My skin burns where it comes into contact with hers, and I ache at the feeling. My legs move restlessly, and I adjust, but she doesn't move her hand. Her eyes stay focused on mine, and I feel a pull towards her, like this is our moment. The one I have been waiting for.

"Sy," she whimpers, a tear escapes her eye, and I bend down. My eyes don't leave hers as my tongue flicks out, catching the salty drop with the tip. Her grip tightens and she pulls me closer, her lips a hair from mine.

"*Ami*," I say breathlessly. I can hear her heart beating, her pulse racing in tune with mine. Her eyes start to close and mine widen. Is this...*no*. This can't be happening.

We have always had an attraction to one another. When we were children, we would practice our kissing, like most children do. But it grew and I found myself wanting more with her, and despite the signs that she does too, we've never acted on it.

I want it—I want *her*—but what about Kass?

Water splashes in the distance and I lean back, her hand dropping from my cheek as we both look up at my brother.

"Well?" I ask. "Did you make it all the way there?" I say with a smirk. Kass loves Amaya, but I don't necessarily think he'd be hurt if we were to do anything. He tends to have the mindset of the Vodian *savages*.

"No." He pouts as he drops down next to us, water flinging in all directions, getting me wet. "I tried though."

"Of course you did," I sigh and stand.

"Where are you going?" Ami asks, sitting up, and I avoid looking at her bare skin.

"I meant to tell you when I came over here, Prince Argent is here. In the palace," I groan and roll my eyes, although I don't know why. He may be annoying, but I also find his lack of decorum...intriguing.

"The Prince of Noterra?" Kass asks, his eyes widening. I nod. "Why?" I shrug and start to walk away, knowing my mother would want me to entertain.

"Who knows, but he's already being a pain in the ass," I yell behind me.

Chapter Five

The Fabricated

I'm not even going to pretend I'm not straining against my pants as I watch the tip of her tongue brush against the other girl's cheek. Her bare chest being caressed by her long, silver hair.

"Who is that?" I whisper to myself. I wonder if her mother knows she has a female lover.

Her brother appears, Prince Kassius if my memory serves me right. Both girls lean away from each other and by the loving look in his eyes, I think that girl and the prince are *together*.

I smirk and adjust my pants as I watch them. I know I look absolutely deranged standing in the trees like this, but I can't stop thinking about her. Although it seems her thoughts are on someone else.

I'll have to change that.

No, Archie. What are you doing?

Sybil rises from the sand, brushing it off her short dress, a dress that wouldn't be allowed in Noterra, before yelling something behind her.

"He's already being a pain in the ass." Her voice is bright and clear, and a small chuckle escapes my lips. She's talking about me.

Her eyes flick over to where I am standing, and I step further behind the tree line. Her brows furrow but she doesn't come closer and instead starts to head back to the palace. I watch her depart for a mere second before turning back towards the other two.

The prince is on top of the other girl, her legs wrapped around his waist. At least I know that he isn't innocent. But what about the princess?

Her innocence is the one I find interesting.

Chapter Six

The Moon

The scream tears through my throat as the silver aether pours from my fingertips. Heat spreads along my skin as shafts of light slam into the targets around me, obliterating them to ash. Sweat beads on my forehead and as the light fades, so does the warmth.

"Wonderful, princess!" His calm voice echoes around the empty chamber, bouncing off the stone walls. My eyes open and I glance around. Smoke billows from equidistant piles of rubbish. Men are already coming through the doors, resetting fresh targets. "Now if only we could get you to focus on a single stream, and not an orb."

"Kalus, is it not more beneficial to destroy all of the enemies around me instead of picking them off one by one?" I counter as I stretch my neck.

"What if there weren't enemies around you, but allies, or innocents? And only one or two of them needed your moonlight? What then? Control, princess. That is why we do this."

"I have control," I spit, rolling my eyes.

"Aim for this one." His hand raises, pointing at a fresh target facing the back wall. I raise my own arm, and he clucks his tongue, "No."

"What *now?*"

"You should not have to raise your arm and point to aim. The aether bends to your will, it is shaped by your wants. Don't let it control you." He steps quietly behind me, and I glare at the target—canvas stuffed with hay and moss, forming the rough shape of a body. Larger than me, but far enough away that aiming with my hand would be easier.

I take a deep breath and focus on the single target. Just the one.

You got this, Sy.

His voice is like a beacon in my head, even though he's still at the laguna. My hand lifts and I brush the crescent moon shaped pendant that keeps me connected to my brother. The sirenstone that makes us one.

I don't move, I don't aim. I just use my will, my desires as Kalus said, and picture the target burning.

Aether shoots out of my fingertips, headed not towards the target, but straight down into the floor and straight into my own chest, following the direction my fingers were facing. My back hits the ground with a *thud* and I gasp. While my own aether would never hurt me, it can still knock me on my ass.

"Princess!" Kalus's voice is shrill as he bends down over me.

I take it back. Kassius laughs in my head before cutting off our connection, but not before I could send him the image of a particularly vulgar gesture. I pull myself up into a sitting position, staring at the unmarred target. Movement catches my eye, and I glance up and to the right, where a thin walkway circles the room. A black robe disappears into the stairwell, and I know my mother just saw me fail.

"Again!" I yell as I rise and mentally aim for the target.

After three hours, I was successful. And by successful, I mean I grazed it at least.

The milky water encompasses me, caressing my skin in a comforting embrace. My limbs tingle, my muscles strained from training, and I curse the fact that my mother called for a family dinner tonight. I dunk my head under the water, opening my lungs so the liquid infiltrates every crevice of my body. A burning spreads through me and I know it's my magic fighting against one another, the small part of me that is a siren mixing with the majority of witch genes in my blood.

I grasp the moon-shaped pendant and hold it tightly, letting the sharp edges prick my skin, tinting the water pink.

Why must life be so hard? I ask the stone, hoping it would give me an answer, but it's my brother who responds.

You are the difficult one, Sy. You should let them help you. Take the elixir, let it help define your magic. He says softly. He doesn't sound like he is at the laguna anymore; his presence is closer.

I don't want to be known as the witch who relied on modern science in order to control herself. I snap back.

Modern science is going to make you stronger. Don't complain. Take the assistance. He chastises and I wish I could slap him.

Says the man who requires the help of no one to access his full range of magic. I release the pendant and break through water, inhaling the fresh air. Water shoots out of my nose as oxygen replaces it and I force a cough. A knock sounds at the door, and I glance at it.

"Your Grace." Daya dips her head as a sign of respect and I nod, gesturing for her to continue. "Your mother has sent for you. Dinner will begin shortly."

"Thank you, Daya," I respond as she departs. So it was her sister Lorna I saw earlier. Daya's hair is slightly darker, more chestnut than golden brown.

I rise, letting the water drip onto the floor as I grab an obscenely fluffy towel. I wrap it around me, before stepping onto the cool stone and into the dressing room.

Chapter Seven

"Where is our esteemed *prince*?" Kass sneers from my left, his fork stabbing into his roast pheasant restlessly. Our mother was stern saying that we couldn't start to eat until the prince arrived, and my brother doesn't mess around with food. I can hear his growling stomach screaming for sustenance.

"He stepped out, but assured me he would be back for dinner, Your Grace," Abel, one of the royal guards, says from his place by the door. His deep skin is glowing in the red torch light, the broad muscles of his chest straining against the leather strap across it. He catches my eye and I wink at him. One good thing about my mother having attractive guards, is that I have no shortage of men to ogle.

Maybe one of these days I'll let them bed me.

"I apologize, Your Grace, for my tardiness." Argent steps through the door, his chest bare like all men in this country. My eyes catch on his long, sleek muscles, and I feel my cheeks redden. He could give Abel a run for his money.

"It is of no consequence, prince. Why have you no guards?" my mother asks, and he takes a seat right across from me. My gaze snaps to the corded muscles in his forearms as he reaches for his wine glass.

"It seems they are single handedly funding your brothels in the city." He smiles and dips his chin as a sign of respect to my mother. My brows furrow and I pick up my fork, stabbing it into a roasted carrot. My mother glares at me as I stick it in my mouth, relishing in the honey glaze.

"Well, please allow our royal guard to escort you from now on," my mother coolly orders as she delicately cuts her meat.

"Forgive me, Your Grace, but I was under the impression that Zivell is a country of peace, one that shouldn't foster fear in it guests?" Kass snorts, covering it up with a cough as he shoves bird in his mouth. Argent doesn't even acknowledge him as he stares at my mother with a questioning gaze.

He's arrogant, I'll give him that.

"While we *are* the safest country, do not mistake that for being without threats. There are many people who wish to see The Divide taken down, and a lot of people who wish to have a new ruler installed in Noterra." My mother's response is slick, sending an oily feeling down my spine.

Is she one of them?

"Be that as it may, I couldn't feel any safer being in the presence of both fire and the moon personified." He's smooth. I find the corner of my mouth twitching as I glance over at Kassius. He seems just as captivated as my slack jawed mother.

"You flatter us, prince. But please allow the guards to escort you until yours decide to vacate our brothels and resume their duties," she instructs before finally digging into her own plate.

"As you wish, Your Grace," Argent responds, picking up his own fork.

"And how long will you be staying with us, Argent?" Kassius asks, stabbing a potato.

"As long as it takes for delegations, Kassius," he responds with an heir of superiority about him.

"Delegations for what?" I ask, piping up.

"That is of no consequence, Moonlight," my mother sneers.

"I feel it is. As the heir to this mighty country, shouldn't I be privy to council matters, *Firelight*?" I say with as much disdain as the queen showed me.

"A marriage alliance between our high lord and one of your ladies," Argent interrupts, no doubt attempting to calm the storm about to wreak havoc in the small dining room. My eyes widen as I gape at him.

"Amaya was right?" I spit, slamming my hands on the table and throwing my chair back. I don't hear it hit the floor, so I assume Abel must have caught it. "You've come to take her?" I yell, leaning forward and staring into his green eyes. My mother flinches and sets down her silverware, preparing for a fight.

"It is not me, *princess*. It is my uncle and your mother who are organizing this," he spits back.

"But you have come to collect, *prince*?" He stands, copying my position by slamming his hands on the table and leaning closer to me, his nose nearly touching mine. The flames on the tall candles wink out, as my mother waves her hand, preventing either of us from starting a fire by knocking them over.

"I am merely an envoy," he sneers. His breath bathes me in the scent of mint and moss. A scent that reminds me of home…

"An envoy who has come to take my best friend from me," I retort, swallowing down the foreign desire.

"None of this is personal, princess. This is politics. Do you think I like the idea of forcing a young girl to marry someone she does not know? Do you think that somehow pleases me in your sadistic view of my character? No. It does not. It makes me *sick*. But I am not the problem here. I am not the one organizing this. My uncle and your mother are," he admits, and I almost feel bad for assuming, but he deserved it.

"Enough! Both of you," my mother snaps. I can feel the heat of her flames digging into my shoulders as she forces me into my seat. Fiery strands wrap around my chest, holding me against the back of the chair and I squirm. "I will not have you two fighting like children. You are both heirs of your respective countries, now act like it!" Argent and I glare at each other, our eyes boring holes in the other as heat snaps at my skin.

I think I might kill him.

"How can you sell Ami off like cattle?" Kassius's voice is soft as he finally speaks up. I'm the outspoken one, he's the timid and quiet brother who rarely shows emotions, but this might be the moment that finally breaks him.

"We need the alliance."

"Why?" I ask.

"Because" my mother responds.

"There is no war brewing. We have no need for ships or money. What is it you want?" I press.

"Stop questioning my decisions and motives, child. When you are queen, you can be a part of these delegations, but until then, mind your business." The fiery whips release my shoulders and I stand.

"I hope your ship sinks to the bottom of the sea and the waterwyvos devour you whole," I spit, albeit childishly, at the prince before storming out of the dining room.

Amaya is in her chambers, lounging on her grand bed in nothing but a dressing robe. She sits up as I storm in.

"What is it?" she asks, her voice full of worry, panic brewing in her eyes.

"They are sending you away, I say breathlessly as I walk straight up to her and press my lips against hers.

Chapter Eight

The Moon

Her lips are hesitant before they are claiming mine in return. Her fingers tear the tether out of my hair, freeing the silver waves, before threading her fingers through the strands. Her lips part and my tongue infiltrates, caressing hers.

Teeth clash as I push her back, climbing on top of her. She moans as I release her lips, trailing kisses down her neck before biting her shoulder.

"Wait—" she whispers. I pull back and stare into her eyes.

"For what?" I ask.

"We can't do this."

"*Why*?" She pushes my shoulders and I slide off the bed.

"Kass."

"Kassius? The man who didn't defend you at dinner? The man who is fine letting Argent take you? The man who is allowing our mother to sell you like an animal?" I yell, spinning around.

"Sy—"

"This has been a long time coming, Amaya," I retort.

"I will not deny I have feelings for you."

"But?"

"But I love your brother."

"I love *you*!"

"You can't!" she snaps back, sliding off the bed to walk over to me. "You can't. I am being wed. You will soon be sent off to wed another. We don't get to fall in love."

"Ami," I plead, grabbing her face.

"No. I can't do this. Not if I am going to leave tomorrow and never see you again."

"We don't know when you're leaving."

"Sybil, the fact still stands that I am leaving."

"You are going to regret this. You are going to regret pushing me away when you are on the other side of the world forced to lay in a man's bed."

"You're probably right, but that doesn't change my answer now."

"And Kassius? Will he get a proper goodbye?"

"Sy, please. Don't make this harder than it needs to be."

"Amaya! Don't pretend this isn't what you want!"

"You don't *deserve* me, Sybil. You aren't *owed* my body. You don't own me. You can't tell me what I want or what to do. I am telling you *no*." My lips part as I stare at her. Gods, what am I doing?

"I'm sorry," I whisper before running out of her room.

My feet slip over the stone as I round the corner and run smack dab into someone's bare chest. Mint and moss wash over me and I push on his arms.

"Excuse you," he snaps as he steps away from me.

"My apologies, *prince*," I hiss, stepping away from him and quickly wiping a stray tear. His fingers wrap around my arm pulling me back towards him.

"Which one of the guards does your mother have to thank for stealing your virtue? My money is on Abel, the one who couldn't keep his eyes off you."

He bites his bottom lip, his green eyes darkening as he leans down.

"What are you talking about? Let go of me!" I rip my arm out of his grasp and step a few feet back.

"Swollen lips and messed up hair. Or was it *that girl*?" he snorts.

"You are out of line!" I yell, brushing hair out of my face.

"I don't care who you fuck, princess, but if you mess anything up in regard to this deal, I will personally make sure your life is hell." He seemingly grows two feet as he towers over me.

"Anytime I am in your presence, I am *already* in hell."

"The feeling is mutual, little moon." He chuckles and I feel heat pooling in my palms.

"Stay away from me," I sneer through gritted teeth.

"Gladly! I can't stand your attitude and lack of respect. I pity any man who is forced to marry you. They'll probably kill themselves out of desperation." The screams erupt from my mouth as I slam my hands into his chest. Silvery sheaths of light explode out of my palms, barreling into his chest. His eyes widen as he goes flying, hitting the wall behind him.

I'm not afraid to admit...

I ran.

Chapter Nine

The Fabricated

She runs. The little tyrant actually runs. She turns down the corner as I stay on the floor.

My spine is aching and the skin on my chest burns from where her aether touched me. Despite the pain and discomfort, I find myself laughing. It comes out as an uncontrollable chuckle as I pull myself to my feet.

Two perfect handprints are burned into my chest. But the skin is already started to regenerate, and I watch as the blistered red turns to a mottled pink, before fading back into my tan.

That's the only good thing about this curse.

I can heal in seconds.

Chapter Ten

The Moon

Breakfast the next day was anything but dull. Amaya wouldn't look at me, she stayed plastered to Kass's side. My mother was too busy reading terms and offers sent by the King of Noterra. And Argent? His unmarred, bare chest was staring right at me as he chowed down on fruit and eggs. His eyes were stuck in a glare as he watched my every move, but he didn't say a single word.

Nobody did.

Silence prevailed as we all ate, until one by one, we all departed.

I don't know why I went where I did, but after I successfully slipped out of the palace without Abel or another following me, I went straight to the Shiny Pearl.

The tall, stone and wood structure blends into the street. Up and down on both sides, different houses and stores sit. They all look identical aside from markers above the door.

This one has a pair of breasts stamped into the wood placard, marking it as a brothel.

Sounds of pleasure and laughter filter out of the open windows, along with the smell of cheap ale and sex. My bare feet step in something sticky as I push the door open, and I nearly gag.

The room is filled with mist as people mingle in various stages of undress. Some are having sex right here in the open, others simply touching each other. Stairs lines both sides of the square room, leading up to private chambers. Red and brown couches and chairs are dotted around, peeking out of the sage scented mist. I step further in, and cold hands brush my bare belly.

I was only wearing a green bandeau and matching skirt, one of my favorite outfits to help combat the heat, and I didn't even question how much of myself was showing.

"Little princess. What is it that we can do for you today?" Another set of hands grab my neck, lifting my head up as a tongue slides down my jaw. I gasp at the feel, my hands clenching at my sides.

"Um," I stutter as the first pair of hands slides down my belly, playing with my waistband.

"What is your taste, Your Grace? Men? Women? *Both*?" A sultry female voice purrs in my ear and I shiver. *Gods*.

"I don't think she knows." A deeper voice whispers. My eyes close as I feel teeth grip my ear lobe, yanking slightly.

"Well let's give her a taste." I am shoved forward, my hands flying down to stop my face from landing in someone's lap. A man laughs and his hands tangle in my hair. I push him off, just to be pulled back up to where another hand slides down my skirt.

"Wait!" I gasp as fingers touch me where only I have ventured before. "Wait!" I say again as I am spun around. Warm lips press into mine before they are ripped away and silence ensues.

Every single person in the room goes quiet and I force my eyes to open.

Dark green irises stare back at me as Argent wraps his hand around a man's throat. The man who just had his hands on me. His lips part as he snarls, shoving the brothel worker away.

"You are going to make ruining you way too easy, princess," he spits, stepping into me. The back of my legs hit the edge of the settee and I grab his arm to prevent myself from falling back. His muscles tense and if I was normal girl I'd probably swoon.

"What are you doing here?" I snap, digging my nails into his flesh.

"Following you," he responds with a wicked gleam in his eye.

"Don't you have delegations with my mother?" I retort, releasing his arm. He catches my hand and yanks me towards the stairs. "Stop!" I yell as he pulls me up and all the way to the fourth floor. The hallway is silent, no noise permeating through the shut doors before he pushes the last one in the hallway open.

A dark room with a bed and fireplace greet us. The fireplace is unlit, thankfully, otherwise it would be too hot. The bed is mussed, blankets thrown around. No color or decorations about.

"What do you want?" I yell.

"What do *I* want?"

"Yes."

"A peaceful day, but instead I was saving you," he groans, running his hands through his cinnamon strands.

"I didn't need to be saved," I mutter.

"Do you know whose hands were touching you?" he spits stepping closer.

"Someone I was getting ready to hire."

"Someone who was going to brag about fucking the princess."

"So? Let him!" I respond, crossing my arms.

"Fine. Let's go get him." He grabs my hand again and yanks me back out of the room. "I'm in need of a whore! Male or female, doesn't really matter!" he bellows as he pulls me down the dark hallway.

"Stop!" I yell and he spins back around.

"Is that really how you want to lose your virginity, princess?"

"Who says I'm a virgin?"

"Are you?" His voice softens in question.

"That's a highly inappropriate question." My brows raise and I stare at him bewildered.

"In Noterra, a women's chastity is a prized possession saved for their husband."

"Well it's not like that here. Fucking is a way of life." His nostrils flare.

"Oh yeah?" He steps into me, his breath cascading over my face.

"Yes," I whisper, breathlessly. I stare into his eyes, my pulse pounding.

"Tell me, little moon. How many times have you partaken in this way of life?" His whisper cascades over my face, sending a chill down my spine.

"Dozens," I say, my voice little more than a whimper.

"Dozens? All the same man? Or was it *women*?" He brushes loose hair off my shoulder, his hand skimming the bare skin. Featherlight touches that leave me aching.

"Both," I whisper. He smiles, his eyes darkening.

"I don't believe you." He leans down, his hand sliding down my back. His lips are barely a hair from mine as I tilt my head up.

"I don't care," I respond before punching him in the jaw.

I run—again. My legs carry me down the stairs, and I almost make it to the second-floor landing before arms wrap around me.

I scream as I am carried through a door into another room, this one with a made bed. I barely have time to think before his lips are slamming into mine.

Teeth, tongue, and gasps of air. His hands dig into my hair as he pushes me back. I grip his wrists, half stuck between pushing him away and holding him closer. My thighs hit the high mattress, and I gasp for air.

"Prove it."

"What?" I barely get the word out as his teeth clamp down on my neck. I scream out as he spins me around.

"Prove to me how much of a *whore* you are," he groans before shoving his hand down the front of my skirt.

His fingers touch me mercilessly. His calloused skin is rough as he rubs the apex of my thighs. I moan as I lean back, his other hand going around my throat, squeezing until only a stream of air can make it through.

His hand slides down through my slit before he sticks one finger *inside* of me. A sharp gasp escapes my lips at the feel of it.

"Oh, little moon." He sighs and pulls his finger out, stepping away from me as I fall forward onto the bed. "What a liar you are." He sighs again and his footsteps recede.

"What?" He looks at me before slowly lifting his finger up and sticks it in his mouth before gloriously, and slowly sucking it clean.

"You have yet to experience the touch of a man, and I won't be your first," he says smoothly before leaving me wet and dumbfounded in the middle of a brothel.

Chapter Eleven

The Fabricated

I shouldn't have done that.

I shouldn't have touched her, and I shouldn't have followed her.

But as I race through the streets, running off steam, I don't feel an ounce of regret.

I don't know what she has or hasn't done, but the feel of her tight heat was enough to make me almost drop to my knees and beg for her.

How pathetic does that make me?

I pick up my pace, turning down another road. Maybe running will get it out of me. Sweat trickles down my neck as the humidity presses in and I take a deep breath.

What is it about her that is screaming for me?

I make it back to the palace and take a cool bath this time. Relishing in the feel of it against my skin, washing away the day.

Washing away her.

Far too soon, I am redressing and walking to the Zivell council chamber where Maeryn awaits. I'm not sure if she prefers to be referred to as Firelight or not, but my uncle calls her Maeryn when we discuss her.

She's sitting at the head of the table, her arms crossed in front of her, watching the door.

"You make being tardy a habit, prince," she says coolly, and I wince. I can see where Sybil got her attitude from.

"Apologies, Your Grace." I bow and then take a seat at the other end of the table. "I was with your daughter in town." Her eyes widen and a frown appears.

"I would appreciate it if you stayed away from Sybil." Her voice is flat, strained.

"I assure you; I mean her no harm. She was showing me downtown," I lie quickly, shifting in my chair.

"You spent all day there yesterday. Did you not explore it enough?" she counters. What is it with this woman?

"There is always more to see with the help of a local," I recover, and she nods, although I can tell she doesn't believe me.

"My daughter is not for sale," She quips.

"I have no intention of trying to buy her." My voice hardens. I can't tell if this is motherly love or power she's expressing.

"Very well, then. Shall we discuss the girl you *are* buying?" She smirks and I feel a challenge brewing.

"I would like to make it clear, Maeryn, that *I* am not purchasing Amaya. My uncle is. I don't like the idea of selling women to keep wars at bay, but I am not yet king. If I was, the Rosenthal's would be butchered and not placated with an eighteen-year-old child. I am merely doing what I am asked."

"Then do it silently."

"I understand the difference in power here, Maeryn. But I will not allow you to speak to me as if I am a child. I am the Noterran envoy, and you will give me the respect I deserve." I straighten my spine and narrow my eyes.

"And you will do well to respect that I am queen here." I don't respond. My irritation growing tenfold. I can't read her, can't tell what it is she is trying to achieve here, but I do know what she wants. I rise, not saying a word and her eyes widen. "Where are you going?" She pushes as I step away from the table. I take a single step towards the door, and I hear her chair slide across the floor. "Wait! I apologize, prince," she says, her voice sounding strained.

I turn back around, taking my seat again. I lean back, throwing an ankle over my knee in a position of relaxation. I know I look arrogant, but I am. I just got what I want.

"Shall we discuss the ships, money, or men first? Or maybe you can enlighten me on what you are preparing for, Maeryn?"

Chapter Twelve

The Moon

Two days pass. Two days of delegating while I hide anywhere but in the palace. I haven't seen Argent again. And I don't want to. He hasn't joined us for dinner.

Amaya and Kassius haven't been seen in two days either. Neither of them has returned to the house, neither of them in any of our normal spots. I feel both angry and heartbroken.

She rejected me. Pushed me away and chose my brother.

And then the prince, the stupid redheaded prince who is here to take my best friend, also made me feel something I've never felt before.

I hate all of them.

I sigh as I dig my fingers into the moss, letting my nails cake up with dirt.

"Everyone in this world was born with half a brain, yet I was cursed with both sides." I groan to myself, slamming my eyes shut as the warm rain drops land on my face. The forest floor is soft against my back, the bright pink orchids filling the air with their sickly scent. My bandeau and skirt are barely concealing my golden skin as I settle against the ground.

I could stay out here forever, and no one would ever know.

Except someone does.

Footsteps pull me from my daydreaming, and I sit up, my body on alert.

"What do you want?" I call out into the fading light streaming between the treetops.

"I am off tomorrow, little moon." His voice is like a cold beverage on a hot, summer day and I hate it. I hate how it makes me feel.

"Good," I spit, gathering my skirts around me.

"You don't want to offer me a proper goodbye?" His voice is both rough and smooth at the same time and it makes me want to stab him.

"If by a proper goodbye you mean shooting aether through your temple, then absolutely. I am more than happy to oblige." I pull myself up and turn to face him, hands at the ready.

I'll play if that's what he wants.

His white linen tunic is open, revealing his bare chest. The same loose black trousers he's been wearing since his arrival. His bare feet digging into the soft forest floor, disrupting it with its foreigner touch.

"Will you miss me?"

"The way the townspeople miss floods, yes," I quip.

"Romantic," he snorts.

"Romancing you is the last thing I would desire."

"You know you think about me," he pushes, and I grit my teeth.

"I don't think about you at all. And I would appreciate you refraining from thinking about me. You can go now," I dismiss him before stepping between the trees and out of sight as quickly as I can.

He doesn't follow me, but I do see the slight swish of a spotted tail in the underbrush by the palace. A tail that doesn't belong to any of the predators here.

I sit on the pier watching the ship sail away. Amaya didn't even say goodbye to me, just to Kassius and my mother. To be fair, I didn't give her a choice. I stayed out of the common areas, keeping to myself.

How do I say goodbye? How do I apologize for throwing myself at her? I don't know what to do anymore.

I didn't see Argent again either.

I was just left alone.

Why do I always feel so alone?

Chapter Thirteen

The Fabricated

My thoughts still linger on her as the ship pulls out of the harbor. Amaya isn't sulking, like I thought she would.

Like I would expect the little heathen to if she were in this position.

Instead, she is propped up on a table, relaxing. Reading a book—no care in the world.

"Are you not sad, my lady?" I ask as I take a seat on the one stool she doesn't have her feet propped up on. She's wearing a sundress, her legs exposed. The Rosenthal's won't appreciate her lack of modesty, although I find it refreshing.

"The day was going to come when the queen grew tired of me. It was only a matter of time," she responds leisurely, barely paying me any notice. I chuckle and lean back.

"What about Kassius?" I press. She still doesn't look up at me.

"Kassius was my first love, but he will not be my last. That is not how it works for women."

"And what about the princess?" Her eyes flick up at me at the mention of her, her brows furrowing slightly.

"She is my dearest friend, and I will always miss her." I raise a brow in question, and she cocks her head. "Is there something you wish to say?" she pushes this time.

"I have nothing to say." I hold my hands up in defeat and smile.

"Then leave me be," Amaya sighs.

"What is it with you women in Zivell? Are attitudes assigned at birth?" She slams her book shut and drops her feet, staring at me.

"What is your problem, Argent? Do you like instigating me?"

"I am not instigating you, Amaya. I am trying to make conversation. We have three days at sea, I'd rather not spend them in silence."

"Alright, then let's talk. Why have you not married?"

"Excuse me?" My mouth gapes as her question surprises me.

"You are twenty years of age, an heir, a male. You should have a bride by now, a queen to rule with you when your uncle passes on," she says quickly, waving her hands around.

"My uncle is young and perfectly healthy, there is no rush for a bride."

"You don't want someone to spend time with?" she presses.

"Well, I have you, don't I?" I smirk and she rolls her eyes.

"I am not your friend, Argent."

"Archie."

"Whatever." Her eyes roll and she leans back against the chair.

"You two are remarkably similar."

"What is your obsession with Sybil?"

"Besides the fact that she is a heathen. A tyrant. A royal pain in the ass-" I start naming off the different descriptors of the woman I can't seem to forget.

"Care to throw in a few more adjectives?"

"I have no obsession with the princess."

"Then why won't you say her name?" Her eyebrow quirks and I find myself dumbfounded. I don't say her name. Ever.

"I have known her all of three days, and in those few days she has done nothing but irritate me." She sighs, props her legs back up, and opens her book.

"Hate and love are a fine line."

"So are intelligence and delusion."

Chapter Fourteen

The Moon

"What do you want, little princess? Do you want freedom? Do you want power? What do you crave? You can have it all, I can give it to you."

It would be so easy to say yes, to give in. His eyes are gray, shadowed. His hair a golden copper. Who is he?

"Who are you?" I ask, reaching forward to touch his cheek.

"I am yours," he whispers.

I gasp as I sit up in bed, soft linens draped around me like a tourniquet. Who was the man? He seemed so familiar, but it seemed like a life that didn't belong to me. I lean against my headboard and shut my eyes.

His hair fell in wavy tendrils to his eyes, that stormy gray filled with anger. He was beautiful, as if he was carved from porcelain. But there was something about him. Something that screamed for me to get out. Or was it even me?

I sigh and reopen my eyes, glaring at the wall in front of me. The glass panes are open, the tall trees brushing the balcony railing. Rain pours from the sky, making the air thick with humidity.

One month has passed since Amaya's departure. Or since Argent bought her as if she were a piece of gold or prized cattle. We have heard nothing from her directly, but we did receive a general piece of mail announcing the new bride of Lord Henry Rosenthal's son, Evreux.

The Rosenthal's are a ruthless bunch, that much I have always known. It is no secret they despise the new order of things, that they have hated the idea of The Divide since its creation a year or two after my birth. While the Rosenthal's are without magic themselves, they are part of a small group of people who want to control us.

Control our magic. Not stifle it, no they hate that the divide does that. What they want is to breed it into their own bloodline.

What they want is to rule.

But they are not of royal blood. Noble, yes, but not royal. And the only way they could sit their privileged asses on the Noterran Throne would be through war. A war I am not sure they would win.

The continent has been at a state of peace for nearly eighteen years, after King Jahara, Argent's uncle, had The Divide created. Segregation was never the plan, but after the civil war decades ago, those with magic in their blood could never trust humans, and vice versa. We were kidnapped and used for breeding, for strengthening bloodlines. Our own countries were ransacked, our royal children stolen in the night.

Now we have peace. We have our side of Viridiana, and they have theirs. I have never crossed the Senaya Sea or The Divide. My father's country, Vodia, sits right in between. A small boat ride from his beaches would have one crossing the unseen barrier. The barrier that would dampen my magic, so I am nothing more than a shell.

Until I am almost human.

My mother has forbidden any of those with magic blood to cross the barrier, as a way to protect us. But there is no telling how many of them were already on that side.

How many Viridiana citizens had aether in their blood and didn't know it?

That is what I feared most. That one day an uprising would occur and any of those who descended from the powerful folk would fight their way to the top.

I only hope that war happens on my mother's watch, and not mine.

"Good!" Kalus exclaims from where he leans over the railing, looking down at the improved training wing. I caved and took the elixir, a small dose every morning to help ignite my magic. It was made of witch's blood, wyvos-ink, and a few toxic herbs. It would kill a human, burn their veins and skin from the inside out, but for me, it makes my aether go wild.

It makes it nearly uncontrollable. The elixir itself is called The Beast. An apt name as it forces one's inner beast to take control. For me, it was the moonlight. For others, it would be something else. If a being such as a wyvos or siren took it, it would allow their other self to take control. Allow extra energy to burn off.

I barely grunt as perfect streams of aether hit each target as Kalus calls them out.

"Send them out!" I snap and face the archway that leads to the barracks. Men in steel armor file out—daggers, falchion swords, and lances dangling from their gloved hands. My mother imbued their weapons to resist my aether specifically, claiming I needed to learn how to fight.

She was probably right.

A circle of lucky sacrifices surrounded me, and my fingers twitched, aching to attack. The first one moved, his spiked lance swinging through the air and barely missing my shoulder. I dropped to my knees as it flew overhead, sending a shaft of aether towards his legs. The force knocked him on his back, and I turned to face the next.

Blade after blade flew through the air along with perfect arcs of silver light. I deflected them all, sending men onto their backs. Men who were trained since they could walk to fight in a future war.

Men who stood no chance.

But despite all the success I had, one got through the aether.

I yelled out as the blade pierced my back right under my shoulder blade. I spun out of the way sending a wave of aether in Abel's direction, but he dodged it.

"Enough!" Kallus yelled from above. I held up my hand, ordering him to stop. Everyone but Abel stepped back.

I reached behind, ripping the dagger out of my skin. Blood trickled down, staining the gray breastband I wore before dripping down my bare back.

"Princess," Abel says with a sigh. He knows I won't give up without a fight.

"No aether. You and me. No interference," I spit, rolling my shoulder. The pain hasn't yet come, but it will once the fighting is over.

"Sybil, you don't have to prove anything." He says softly so only I can hear him.

"You're right. I don't have to prove anything. But that revelation won't save you." With a snarl, I launch myself at him.

He blocks my blade with his forearm guard, the leather taking the brunt of the force. He spins out of the way, and I trip. Before crashing to my knees, I catch myself.

My arm snakes up, my dagger hitting his falchion. I can feel him holding back, his strength barely affecting me.

"Don't hold back!" I scream as I slide the dagger down and nick his hand. He rips the helmet and face guard off, revealing pointed teeth stretched into a grin. The metal hits the stone floor with a ringing that echoes through my ears.

"As you wish," he snarls before swinging his sword through the air.

Chapter Fifteen

The Moon

"He should be whipped just for touching you!" My mother's voice bellows as the mender stitches my wounds. I managed to block most of his attacks, but not without getting a few more slices. Though I will say, Abel looks worse off. "What have I told you?"

"Mother, you wanted me to train. I am training. If they went easy on me, I would never learn," I muse as I fight against the pain.

"Abel is the head of the queensguard, and he is now covered in stitches."

"Scars are attractive," I quip, and she spins to face me.

"Moonlight, this is not a joking matter. One inch to the right and he would have gotten your heart." She had the audacity to look even the smallest bit worried.

"*Sybil*," I correct. "And do you not trust his capabilities? He would never kill me. He knew what he was doing, and he knew it would be a flesh wound. As did I when I carved his abdomen up like a fish." My voice is laced with humor, and she rolls her eyes, dropping into the settee in front of me. Her red hair is loose for once, billowing down her back in waves.

"I am done, Your Grace," the mender says, gathering his supplies. He doesn't spare me a glance before bowing and making a hasty exit. I roll my shoulder, feeling the stretch of skin.

"No more."

"No more, what?" I ask, slipping my shirt over my breastband.

"No more beast." My eyes widen and I quickly rise, biting back a wince.

"You are the one who was forcing me to take it! You are the one who told me I needed to grow stronger. You are the one who *made* it!" I yell, my blood nearly boiling.

"And it is affecting your mind!" she yells back. "Child of mine, I see so much untapped strength inside you, but becoming reliant on potions is not going to help you." Her voice softens and I scoff.

"I cannot believe you. You pressure me into taking the elixir and then fault me for using it. You cannot have it both ways, mother." I stomp my way to the door, my bare feet slapping the ground.

"If I hear of you taking more, Moonlight, I will strip you of your aether." I pause, my hand resting on the door frame.

"You wouldn't," I whisper.

"I would."

"That would be a fate worse than death." I say, spinning back around.

"I would rather you be dead than useless," she declares, before grabbing a letter off her pile of correspondence. I don't respond. I swallow the lump in my throat and leave her office, headed straight for the tree.

Black hair, coiled in tiny curls. Blue eyes that rival mine and match the sea as if the deep waters were housed in her irises. Her nose is small, freckles spattered across her pale skin. She looks sad. As if her heart is broken.

"What is making you so sad?" I ask her, but she can't hear me. Her hand rests on the mirror in front of her, a single tear trailing down her cheek.

"I don't want to be here anymore, mama," she whispers.

"Ow!" I yell as I'm poked and prodded.

"I apologize, Your Grace," the mender responds but doesn't stop his stabbing. I feel the pinprick again and bite my lip. "You should begin to feel better shortly," he supplies as he pulls my shirt back up.

"Is it infected?" I ask as I slide off the exam table.

"Not at all, Your Grace," he says softly as he sets the tools in a basin. "It is better to be cautious. I have injected your wound with a mix of poppy root and calendula to help with swelling. Your stitches should be ready to come out in a sennight. There will be a scar, but with a balm of everlasting flower and lavender, it should fade with time."

"Thank you," I whisper as I head towards the door, but something stops me. "Ser," I start.

"Yes, Your Grace?" He turns to face me, his wrinkled brows furrowing in question.

"Do you by chance have a tea or balm that aids in developing visions?"

"Have you been having dreams again?" he questions. I nod. "We could give you some herbs that deepen your sleep, it may help."

"I would like to be able to recall certain visions so that I may better understand them."

"You know that is not possible. You must strengthen your gift; herbs cannot do that for you." His face softens as he rests his hands on the exam table between us.

"There is an elixir for my aether, why not my sight?" I press.

"Some things do not have an easy way out. Some require training and willpower." I look down, pondering. I'll just need to practice then.

"Thank you," I murmur, finally taking my leave.

Chapter Sixteen

The Fabricated

"What is wrong with you?" His irritated voice breaks through my thoughts and I roll my eyes.

"Nothing," I spit, unsheathing my sword.

"Could have fooled me. Ever since you came back with Amaya, you have been distracted."

"Pardon me for not enjoying the act of buying a young girl just because you decided it was time to marry." The sound of steel hitting steel echoes around the training ring as our swords clash.

"Would you have me marry one of the many woman who have vied for my hand?"

"I don't really care who you marry, Ev. But I am curious why you wanted her, why you wanted someone all the way from Zivell. There are so many countries between us and them. Tatus, Dorin, gods you could even go to Khailes," I mutter as I spin on my back heel, avoiding his strike. I feign to my right just as he lunges, only to sidestep to my left, the blade coming close to his ribs.

"Hey! Watch it!" he yells.

"Defend your organs. One quick jab and you are done for," I instruct, widening my stance in preparation to go again.

"And pray tell, my prince, why must I learn to fight when my father has men hired to do just that in my behalf?"

"One day—" I start as I swing towards his neck, he deflects, but not easily; his face turning red as he strains against me— "you will find yourself in a position where your guards are not around. Do you want to fall victim to traitors and enemies, or do you want to one day be Lord Rosenthal and command the men your father hires?" I press. Evreux is privileged, his life easy. Given that his father is the richest noble in Noterra, he has wanted for nothing his entire life. I can say the same for myself, but being able to protect oneself was something my parents instilled in me from a young age, well through my uncle has they had very strict instructions for how I would be raised. And when they passed just eighteen years ago, something they knew was going to happen, I never wanted to feel as if I was unprotected.

Even though their deaths had nothing to do with traitors and savages, it was a choice they made to better than realm. To make it safer for the newest generation.

To make it safer for me.

His blade slices through my trousers, nicking my thigh. I glance down at the blood welling up, already soaking through the thin material.

"Apologies," he sneers as he sheathes his blade and retreats to the corner for refreshments. I groan, ignoring the pain radiating down my leg. It only takes two beats of my pulse for the skin to begin knitting itself back together, but he can't see that.

No one can.

"We are done for today. I am tired."

"You are distracted."

"I just told you I wasn't," I protest, grabbing my own mug of water.

"My annoying little wife seems to think it has something to do with the Zivellian Princess." His mouth is hidden by the wood of his mug, but I can see the smirk crinkling the edges of his eyes.

"Your wife needs to mind her own business. Besides," I say softy, "she's wrong. I am glad to be away from that little terror. She had enough attitude to fuel a thousand torches."

"Which she could with her aether."

"Not on this side of The Divide," I respond.

"The Divide dampens, Arch, not destroys. She could still use her moonlight over here."

"I guess we will never find out."

"Your Grace." A gruff voice echoes across the courtyard, and I glance over to see one of the royal guard bowing before me.

"Yes?"

"The king requests your presence." I nod once, dismissing him.

I leave Evreux to his own entertainment, stalking through the halls until I enter the throne room. The red and silver throne is a direct contrast to the white marble walls and floor, a dark beacon in a room of light. I always hated it, but it's been the royal seat for as long as the scholars remember. I walk past the dais and to the left, where I enter the council chamber.

My uncle is sitting at the head of the table, his salt and pepper hair tied back into a knot. He glances up at me and pauses his writing.

"Archie, anything?" he asks as I step up to the table. I pull the chair adjacent to him out, dropping into its lush cushion.

"He deflected."

"I expected as much." He sighs, leaning back. "It's been four months since you returned with the girl, and yet we have learned nothing. What is Henry up to?"

Chapter Seventeen

The Fabricated

Branches and thorns rip at my ribs as I run through the underbrush. A growl reverberates through my throat as flashes of the little tyrant flick through my mind.

I can't stop thinking about her. Can't stop dreaming about her.

What is it that is drawing me towards her?

I launch myself off a boulder, flying through the air, before all four of my paws hit the forest floor. The growl grows into a roar as I scream into the night.

Cursing myself for ever going to Zivell in the first place.

Four months. It's only been four months.

But it feels like we have been apart for a lifetime.

Chapter Eighteen

The Moon

"You cannot make me!" I yell in the council room, my voice echoing throughout the vaulted ceilings. Kassius sits in one chair, my mother's councilmen filling the others besides the head of the table.

Where my mother sits.

"I can do whatever I please," she retorts skimming a parchment filled with ink.

"Dorin, mother? A desert. A desert without trees or wildlife, or *aether*." My voice growing in volume.

"Prince Bastian has grown into an attractive young man. Only five years older than you and has already been named his father's hand. He is a fine choice."

"You always said you didn't want me to leave Zivell," I argue, gripping the back of the chair I dramatically threw myself out of at the news.

"Dorin is a safe and respectable country."

"It is a wasteland," Kassius mumbles and our mother shoots him a look.

"You are not marrying me off," I grind out staring into her eyes.

"You will marry before this year is up, Moonlight. You are my heir, but as of yet, the line of succession ends with you. You need children to ensure our blood remains on the throne here," she presses, her voice filled with diplomacy.

"Let me stay here," I beg. "Please, mother."

"What if you marry Bastian and you both reside here? I can give you one of the small palaces by the laguna as your dowry, where you guys can reside until you take my place," she offers. It's a compromise, one she doesn't make often, but I do not want to marry.

"I do not want to marry for duty, mother." My voice comes out strained.

"Then find someone worthy of your hand whom you can love if that is so important to you." My lips part in shock as I stare at her. Murmurs start around the chamber, rising in volume. "Enough!" she yells, and everyone goes silent.

"Are you serious?" I whisper.

"You will begin a marriage tour. Every country on *this* side of The Divide will send their most eligible men. You can choose from them." My hands loosen and a small smile plays at the corner of my lips.

"Thank you, mother."

"Six months. You have six months to get engaged. If by then you still have not found a match, Bastian will be your husband." I nod, eager to buy myself time. "Now, can we continue?" she says as she looks back down at the parchment. I pull my chair out and take it, smiling at the small win.

"Where are we with the men from Noterra, Your Grace?" My mother's Master of Arms speaks from my left.

"They are doing what I commanded them to," she says offhandedly.

"Which is?" he presses.

"Staying put," she spits, turning towards our Master of Coin.

"What is the dowry he's offering?" my mother asks, changing topics.

"The Prince of Dorin?" he responds, confusion etched into his face.

"No, Orin. The King of Sesperial." My eyebrows raise and my eyes widen as we all turn to look at her. Sesperial is a continent *far* from Viridana. One we know about as it is the only continent even remotely close to us that does not know or believe in magic. A country we have been warned to stay clear of., If they found out about us and our aether, they might try to take it for themselves. It's a fairly technologically advanced country for having no aether to assist. While I have never seen it myself, I have learned about it in my many books about the world.

The country itself is almost a three-month journey south. A journey that passes rough seas and the rumors of rabid waterwyvos ready to sink any ship that crosses them.

So why is my mother consulting with their King about a dowry if she's always told us to stay clear?

"What are we being paid for by Sesperial?" I question and lean forward.

"They have a daughter. She is sixteen as of now," she responds, looking at Kassius.

"How do you know this?" he asks.

"I saw her, and then sent a raven."

"A raven across the sea, Your Grace? Are you sure it even made it to him?" my mother's hand asks with a gasp.

"Someone responded." She shrugs and returns her gaze to our the coinmaster.

"Over a million gold, Your Grace." A smile spreads across her face.

"Send an acceptance. We shall greet the princess here in six months' time. It seems both of my children are getting married this year."

Chapter Nineteen

The Fabricated

"Are you serious?" I yell as I pace the throne room. My uncle is sitting quietly on the dais, his hands resting in his lap. "How long?"

"In three months' time it seems," I scoff and laugh.

"Would that alliance be a threat?" I press, crossing my arms.

"One between Dorin and Zivell wouldn't entirely be a threat, except for the fact that it is one between both sides," he muses, his eyes wandering.

"I know The Divide is there to prevent another civil war, but is combining blood lines really an issue?" I ask, stepping closer.

"Someone with the power that Sybil has should be careful with who she marries. Marrying just anyone could start a war, one she would be a pawn in," I scoff again.

"That tiny, little devil wouldn't let anyone control her."

"Anyone?" His eyes flick back to mine.

"What are you saying?"

"I am saying that magic should marry magic, and you, my heir, have not yet claimed a bride." My mouth drops open in shock. Me? Marry *her*?

"In three months, Sybil and Bastian will wed. They will have powerful little children that could very well propel Dorin into being one of the most powerful countries in Viridiana. While I have no concern the King of Dorin would start a war, Bastian is a wild card. We do not know what it is he cares for; what his agenda as king would be." My uncle stands and walks down the dais before stopping in front of me.

"You want peace, Archie. You want comfort. You want an easy life, and getting married to Sybil before she has a chance to marry someone else can achieve that. I won't force you to have heirs, at least not yet, but someday."

"You do not know her!" I snap, pacing. "She has the attitude of a spoiled child and the manners of a peasant."

"She is beautiful. She is powerful. And by all accounts, she is more royal than you."

"I am the High King's heir!"

"You have noble blood in half of you. You are the second son's child. You are only the heir because I refused to marry. But she, *Sybil*, is the princess of two of the most aether-fueled countries. She is a witch with the power of the moons. Her mother is Maeryn, fire in the form of a woman." I hold up my hand.

"I know who she is," I spit.

"Then convince her to choose you. Her mother is giving her a choice. She is letting her choose her husband. If she does not fall in love with another or make a choice for herself, Bastian will become the consort of two countries. Two countries we could utilize."

"What are you preparing for, uncle?" I ask, stepping closer to him.

"I am preparing for the day that someone decides peace isn't enough."

Chapter Twenty

The Moon

It took eight months after her departure, before we got a letter from Amaya. Or, at least my brother did. She married a man named Evreux who she says is far from kind. He isn't abusive, thankfully, but he's possessive and has made sure to show everyone who she belongs to.

She is already with child and has been since their wedding night. She thinks it's a girl, but without a mender with abilities, she won't really know what it is until it comes out in a fortnight or so.

Kass disappeared for a few days, and I feel as if he went to Noterra to see her. Mother wouldn't care, she wouldn't even notice. He probably shifted into a bird or something and made the trip as quick as possible. When I saw him again, he was heartbroken and refused to talk. I can't imagine being eighteen—I guess nineteen now—and pregnant. I can't imagine being nineteen, pregnant, and away from everyone I have ever known.

My mother never heard from the King of Sesperial, which was a relief. We have no idea if his daughter is on her way, or if Kassius is actually engaged.

My mother is waiting the remaining two months before questioning it. The same remaining two months I have on my marriage tour. If I don't find someone, Prince Bastian will become my husband.

I groan as I stare at the line of men begging for my favor. My mother is forcing me to endure interviews of potential suitors in the throne room. While I am glad she's allowing me a choice in the man I get shackled to, getting married is the last thing I want.

A lanky, elderly man walks up to the dais of vines before bowing with his arm across his chest. His cloak is of fine quality, marking him as a nobleman or wealthy merchant. His balding head and pockmarked skin do nothing for me, though. I groan inwardly as I realize my mother sent most of these men as punishment. She's getting just as tired as I am.

"Your Grace, it is an honor to finally see the great beauty in person." I snort and his eyes widen before he continues, "Lord Masavey, Your Grace. I am one of the wealthiest merchants in all of Tatus." I was right. "I own several manors that you could enjoy, as well as groves of fruit trees for frolicking—"

"Do I look like one who enjoys frolicking, my lord?" I respond, cocking my head to the side as I cross my legs. My green dress parts, exposing my thigh all the way to my hip. His eyes catch the movement, and he swallows – hard.

"Well, it is something most women enjoy," he stutters.

"I promise you, my lord, I am not like most women." My eyes narrow and I suck on my teeth.

"That I can see, Your Grace," Lord Masavey chokes out, his face growing red.

"What titles besides Lord does he hold?" I ask, glancing up at Abel who is standing to my left with a scroll.

"None, Your Grace," he responds.

"Thank you for your time, Lord Masa-something," I say softly and nod in the other guard's direction. The lord is ushered out with protest on his tongue, but I pay him no mind. I hear soft murmurs of surprise around the room before a deep voice pipes up.

"Your Grace, what an honor to finally see the great beauty—" My head whips over to face Argent as he kneels before the dais.

"What are you doing here?" I snap, louder than I expected.

"Is this not a chance to plead for your hand in marriage?" he snickers as he stands, his teeth biting into his bottom lip, like always.

His hair has been sheared, cropping it close to his head. His skin is just as tan as before, but he looks dirty. He's wearing a beige button down with brown trousers. His boots have dirt caked on them, and he has two swords strapped to his back.

"I am going to assume based on your appearance that you smell of bird poop and sea. Am I correct?" I snort and lean back on the dais, uncrossing my legs and exposing more skin. He doesn't hide his admiration of my body and instead lets his eyes ravish me.

"Sea yes, but the bird poop has been replaced with manure." He smirks, revealing a dimple.

"I see. No, thank you." I lean forward, letting my off-shoulder sleeves droop ever so slightly. "I think I'm done for today," I announce, much to everyone's demise. Angry groans and murmurs spread across the room as people are ushered out by armed guards. They'll have to return tomorrow to plead for my hand. Although, I won't be giving it to any of them.

"Your Grace." Abel offers me his hand and I take it as I rise, stepping down the three steps to the floor. I release his hand and cross my arms in front of me.

"Thank you for your time, prince. Have a nice day." I push past him and his arm snakes around me, spinning me until my hands come up to his chest. Abel's hand grabs his arm and I raise my fingers slightly, dismissing him.

"I missed you, little moon," he whispers.

"I don't believe that for an instance, prince." I respond softly, tilting my head up slightly, exposing my neck.

"No? Want me to show you?"

"Not particularly."

"Ahh, so nothing has changed then?" he retorts, and I untangle myself from his arms, smoothing hair away from my face.

"I'll have you know that things have definitely changed in that aspect. You showed me what I could experience, and it made my hungry. And there are a lot of men *and* women eager to feed a princess." I step away from him towards the double doors, leading out to the hallway.

His calloused hand wraps around my neck, holding me against him as he squeezes not-so-gently.

"Who?" he growls in my ear before rubbing his nose along my jaw.

"Too many to name." My words come out breathlessly and his hand tightens.

"I will find out and—"

"Do what, prince? Fight someone for touching something that does not belong to you?" I croak.

"You may not belong to me, but I can still claim you."

"You cannot claim someone who is not freely given." My hand reaches up to his, letting my aether burn him. He releases me with a yelp, his dark eyes staring intensely into mine. "Have a lovely day, prince." I dip my chin respectfully before leaving the throne room. Abel's glaring face close behind.

Chapter Twenty-One

The Fabricated

Anger and annoyance. That's what I feel as I watch her sashay her way out of the hall, every man in the kingdom staring after her. Those bare legs nearly made me combust.

I am here for duty. For my uncle, but I forgot what she smelled like. Honey and coconut with the underlying earthiness of moss. Her hair loosely waved; the silver nearly incandescent in the torchlight that matched her aether. But as soon as she crossed the threshold, they extinguished.

The room didn't completely darken, the open windows allowed sunlight to filter through, the golden rays a contrast to the sharp silver. The sunlight that was just enough for me to see the deep purple line on her shoulder blade.

A scar, a fresh one.

I bite the inside of my cheek at the raging feelings inside me.

I must convince her to marry me. I must convince her to choose me. And then I must convince myself that this is for the better. This is for the good of the realm.

I pop my knuckles before stalking after her, hellbent on seeing where the little princess goes.

Chapter Twenty-Two

The Moon

"How can she already be pregnant?" he yells as he paces the length of my room.

"Well, I am assuming they were required to consummate their marriage months ago, Kass. She's due any day now."

"This is bullshit. Insanity." He throws his arms in the air and glares at me.

"This is life."

"She never should have gone. We could have gotten married."

"Father would kill her in a heartbeat to free you up for a princess. You know that." I sit up, softening my eyes.

"What about you, huh?'

"What about me?"

"Any potential suitors?" He pushes and I turn away.

"Half of them are older than our mother's mother, and the other half barely could hold my gaze. I will not marry someone who is scared of me."

"Why not? Could be fun?"

"That's not the kind of fun I want."

"There are plenty of brothels. Although I hear you frequent them quite often."

"A princess gets lonely."

"A princess will get pregnant," he snaps back.

"So be it. Maybe then I won't have to marry." I shrug.

"*Sybil.*" His voice is thick with warning, and I look back at him.

"What?"

"You're fighting this," he says.

"As are you."

"No. I leave for Vodia in less than a month, Sy." I shoot off the bed and step towards him.

"No. That's impossible. We don't turn nineteen for another two!" My voice cracks as I get close to him.

"Mother is sending me early; she says I am disturbing the peace."

"Kassius, you can't leave me too."

"Come with me," he pleads, grabbing my hands.

"You know I can't."

"Do it anyway. Father would welcome you with open arms. You were always his favorite."

"Into a country I can't access for more than five hours?"

"Sybil—"

"No. My place is here unless I marry outside the country. Mother made that clear."

"There is always Bastian," I groan and pull my hands away.

"I am not moving to that desert of an island. They don't even have lakes or beaches. It's sand and cacti. They cover every inch of their skin to prevent burns."

"It wasn't that bad when we visited." He smiles.

"That's because you slept with half the ladies," I quip.

"There is always Archie."

"No. I am not marrying that egotistical maniac."

"You protest too much."

"And you not enough," I snap back.

Chapter Twenty-Three

"These gifts are not necessary, prince."

"They aren't from me," I respond, disinterest lacing my voice like venom.

"And what does your uncle want from me now? I have no more maidens in the palace for sale." I roll my eyes.

"I am not here to buy a maiden, Maeryn."

"You cannot have my daughter."

"It seems you reiterate that every time I am in your presence, although I have shown no desire to take her." I straighten my back and lean forward. "Why did you sell Amaya to the Rosenthal's?"

"Why were you their liaison when I expected the lord's son?" she answers with a question.

"My uncle asked me to mediate. You didn't answer my question."

"They needed a bride for Evreux."

"He could have anyone."

"But he wanted Amaya." Her gaze holds mine and I finally understand her irritation about her daughter.

"They wanted the princess, didn't they?" She swallows and leans back.

"Sybil is not permitted to leave the country."

"Why do they want a princess? That is above his station." My hands grip into fists. What is this I feel? Protection? A sense of protecting someone who doesn't want me. I claimed her, even if I can't actually do that. She would skin me alive if I tried.

"Who wouldn't want my daughter? She's powerful. She's beautiful."

"She has an attitude," I mutter and swear I see a ghost of a smile cross her face.

"Why are you here?"

"I came for answers."

"Did your uncle send you?" I don't answer because he didn't. I didn't even tell him I was leaving yet, nor did I bring along any guards. I bought my passage on a merchant ship, hiding my identity.

He wanted me to steal the princess's heart, and that's what I am doing.

"You trade a girl for ships, money, and men. Yet I haven't seen any of them leave Noterra on their journey here. Meaning you didn't get what you paid for? You brokered a deal with a lord instead of working with the king directly. You only spoke to the Rosenthal's until my uncle caught wind and intervened. What are you planning for?" I stand, letting my height intimidate her. Not that anything could.

"I am planning for a future. A future where my daughter can rule in peace. A future where we don't have to watch our backs."

"Your country is at peace! There are no wars to be had or to protect her from. *Unless* you are preparing for one we don't know about?"

"I don't answer to you. Anything I do is to protect my daughter. *My* heir. I won't explain it to you." She rises and motions towards the door. "You can find housing in town, you are not welcome to stay here."

I scoff and exit the room, knowing I needed to find her before it's too late. Before the recklessness leaves my body and is replaced with sanity.

And the fact that I found her in the Shiny Pearl again made that recklessness grow tenfold.

Chapter Twenty-Four

Warmth fills my body as I let him touch me, let him explore. His lips close around my nipple as his hands torture me.

"Don't stop," I whimper as I arch my back.

"Yes, my princess," he whispers back, his teeth grazing my sensitive skin. I can feel the warmth growing, pooling, deep in my belly. I'm so clo—

"What is going on in here?" Someone yells loudly and I sit up, smacking my head against the man whose name I already forgot. Pain shoots through my temples as I blink up at the person who entered.

I gasp as I pull the blanket around me.

"Ser, you must leave. This is a private room."

"You are dismissed." He waves at the gentleman, who glances at me for confirmation. I nod once and sigh, settling against the headboard. "And I thought you were lying."

"What do you want, Argent?" I snap, closing my eyes as the pounding pain infiltrates my head.

"*Archie*. I was just minding my own business when I heard your voice. Seems like an unseemly place for a princess to be."

"Oh, save it, prince!" I yell as I look back up at him.

"I already warned you."

"You warned me what?"

"That I claimed you."

"What are you, a dog? You can't *claim* me." His eyes crinkle as if he's laughing at an inside joke.

"Too bad, little moon. I already did." He saunters forward, ripping his shirt over his head and throwing his swords on the floor. My lips part and my brows furrow as I stare at him walking towards me. He places his hands on either sides of my hips, leaning down so his nose brushes mine.

"If it's pleasure you want, you'll get it from me."

"Fuck off—" His lips slam into mine as he rips the blanket off of me. His fingers dig into my thighs as he yanks me down the bed, settling my thighs on either side of his. "Stop—" I yell against his lips, his fingers squeezing hard enough to bruise.

"You can make me, little moon. You are just choosing not to." He stops kissing me, his eyes meeting mine in question. I flick back and forth between the two emerald irises, my brain scrambling to think.

Fuck it. What do I have to lose?

I grab his face, pulling him back to me. I arch my back, letting my breasts graze his bare chest, and his answering groan lets me know that was the right move. His teeth pierce my lip, and I can taste the blood as it pools in my mouth. His tongue laps it up and I am both utterly disturbed and aroused.

"Have only hands been inside of you, little moon?" he whispers against my neck, and I fidget under him. "Answer me."

"Yes," I force out as he nips at my shoulder.

"Good girl," he responds before gripping the sides of my neck again, his fingers cutting off my oxygen. His free hand undoes his trousers, pushing them down and freeing him. My mouth dries at the sight of his length—of his thickness—throbbing. Corded veins wrap around the pink skin that's hardened more than I thought possible. I dig my nails into his hand, gasping for the smallest stream of air as he leans down.

He rubs against me, and I whimper as his teeth graze my ear.

"I want you to break just for me, little moon," he whispers before slamming into me. Lights spark behind my shut eyes and a silent scream escapes my lips as I feel everything inside me tear. Pain and pressure, stretching and ripping and then—

Euphoria.

The friction, the movement. I can feel my toes curl, heat pooling in my belly. I feel a sensation that I have never felt before as he slams into me over and over again.

I fight to inhale, my head growing dizzy, but he doesn't relent. He keeps moving at a pace inhuman as he takes everything I have. As I freely give it to him.

As I let him ride me into oblivion.

The orgasm hits before I am prepared, and he releases my neck just as I scream. Gasping for air, I clutch onto his neck, pulling him down against me. His fingers move to my hips, digging in as he picks up the pace. His breath is hot against my aching neck as he groans.

The rubbing of his pelvis, the pressure of him inside of me, it's too much. Another release barrels through me and he catches my scream with a kiss before, he too, comes undone, spilling inside of me.

His body collapses on top of me, our breathing ragged.

"I think I'll keep you," he says before nuzzling into my neck.

Chapter Twenty-Five

The Fabricated

Fuck. Fuck. Fuck.

I didn't mean to do that, but when I found her at the Shiny Pearl? Found her below that disgusting man who no doubt has more diseases then a wild animal? Rage overtook me. I had to have her. I had to before I left Zivell.

Before I left her.

But she is not mine to leave. I both can't stand her and can't stay away from her.

I can't force her to marry me, but I ruined her. I aided in her ruin and now I was going to run away with my tail between my legs. I came here for one purpose. I came here for *her*.

And now I am running away.

I left before she woke, running through the trees. The brush of the foliage against my ribs, against my legs.

I just kept running until I forgot who I was.

Chapter Twenty-Six

The Moon

"Stop! Please! I am not her! I am not my mother!" Her scream echoes through my mind as I see blood. I see ripped fabric and fingernails cracking as the mystery girl tries to get away. "I am not—"

I awoke with a start. The name she screamed fading from my mind as soon as my eyes opened. It seemed so real. As if that terror was echoing around the room. As if I could feel it.

I fell asleep on top of Argent, his fingertips running up and down my spine as my cheek was pressed against his chest. The sound of his pulse, the warmth of his skin. I didn't want to, but I couldn't help it. I was so tired, and he felt...

He felt like home.

Why did I allow myself to do this? Allow myself to give the last piece of me to *him* of all people. I don't know what it was, but when I saw him this morning, kneeling before me, I couldn't breathe. Couldn't think.

It took everything in me not to throw myself at him. I remembered the way he felt, the way he kissed, the way he touched me before disappearing, and now I gave him every part of me.

And when I awoke, he was gone.

What did I expect?

I blink groggily as I look around the room. A single torch is lit by the door, barely illuminating the small space with yellow light.

"Argent?" I say softly, but no response comes.

I dress quickly, before padding out into the hallway. The sounds of pleasure radiates from shut doors as I quickly make my way to the stairs. My gaze snags on a mirror hanging on the wall and I gasp.

My lips are swollen, the bottom one cut with dried blood around it. Bruises line my neck like a collar where his fingers touched me. I rip up my skirt and see matching bruises along my hips, my undergarments nowhere to be seen.

I should feel repulsed, but all I feel is...free. A laugh escapes my lips and I drop my skirts, wincing as I feel my insides adjust.

I run all the way home in the dead of night, barely sneaking past the guards as I get to my room.

The bath water is hot as I sink all the way in, my eyes adjusting to the feel of it. My lungs ache, both from disuse and from his hands cutting off my oxygen. My face breaks through the surface and I inhale deeply, relishing in the feel.

I sit up and let my head rest on the back of the tub, the boiling water releasing tension in my muscles. The water is tinged pink, no doubt from the blood between my thighs. Eucalyptus leaves float along with bubbles, filling the bathing room in the scent of earth and cinnamon. Spicy and deep, comforting.

I close my eyes, letting my mind wander.

The throne room is cold, everything tinged red. Rose petals scattered around the marble floors, looking like splattered blood.

"Just let her go." A familiar voice echoes around me, and I spin, trying to find the source. Trying to find him.

"I want one thing. Give it to me and I'll free her."

"Take it!" A shrill scream pierces my ears and I clamp my hands over them.

"Little moon!" I shoot up, water splashing over the edge of the tub, soaking the floor. His hands rest on my shoulders, and I realize I'm shaking. What am I seeing?

"Argent?" I say softly as I look up at him. His hand cups my cheek and I push him away, standing in the tub so that I am as eye level as I can be. "You left me." I spit before stepping out of the water.

"I had to ensure my guards weren't tearing apart your beautiful country in search of me." His eyes widen slightly. He's lying.

"You could have woken me up," I retort, wrapping a towel around myself.

"You were passed out and seemed at peace. I didn't want to ruin that for you." I spin around, facing him. His soft face, his sweet eyes.

"You left me," his hands fall to his sides and his brows pinch together.

"Little moon, I'm sorry." He steps up, wrapping his arms around me, holding my wet body against him.

"Don't leave me again," I whisper, and he nods against my head. Where is this girl coming from? This girl who needs this...*man* to make her feel whole? Is it the vision? The screams that keep echoing through my head that makes me need him. Need comfort?

"I have to return to Noterra eventually. I am just here doing business for my uncle." He clears his throat as if he's thinking.

"When?"

"A few days at most. But preferably as soon as possible." I pull back, looking into his eyes.

"Take me with you."

"What?" His eyes widen, shock spreading over his face. "Are you serious?"

"Take me with you. Take me to Noterra. Take me out of this country," I plead, gripping his shirt with my hands.

"You don't want to go to Noterra, princess. It's a cold and sterile place made warm by only my uncle's presence. Court wouldn't know what to do with you. You're too wild in comparison to the Noterran women," I scoff and attempt to step out of his arms.

"Never mind. Go back to your boring hags."

"I don't want to." Regret passes through his eyes as if he is fighting some inner demon.

"But you won't take me with you?"

"If I take you with me, then they will all expect a wedding," he presses.

"Then let there be one."

"You want to get married? You beautiful little tyrant, we just met," he jokes, a laugh escaping his parted lips.

"No, we met many years ago. Multiple times." I roll my eyes.

"I thought you didn't remember," he says with a smirk.

"Of course I remember, I just hated you."

"Past tense?"

"No, I still hate you." I suck my lower lip between my teeth, biting down. I wince as I reopen the wound he inflicted with his unusually sharp canines.

"You didn't seem like you hated me a few hours ago." A shiver runs down my spine as his tongue catches a water droplet on my cheek.

"Argent—"

"Archie."

"*Argent,*" I repeat. "I have to marry. It's either some elderly lord who was old when my mother was a babe, or a child that I have no desire to touch. *Or* the

Prince of Dorin, but I don't really want to move there. Although my mother did say he could move here." My voice trails off.

"So I'm a last resort?"

"You're my best option."

"Wow, little moon. That almost sounds like a compliment."

"Don't get used to it." I rest my forehead on his chest, my hands gripping the lapels of his tunic tighter, pulling him closer. "How did you even get in here?" I ask, leaning back.

"The window." He smirks, his dimple exposed.

"Keep doing it," I whisper as I release my elbows, the towel falling. I rise up on my toes, wrapping my arms around his neck.

"As you wish," he whispers against my lips before taking me to the floor.

Chapter Twenty-Seven

The Fabricated

Less than a day. That's all it took to get the little princess to beg me for a wedding. To beg for my hand.

I should feel guilty—repulsed—in the ease in which I tricked her.

But I don't.

For once in my life, I am happy.

Chapter Twenty-Eight

The Moon

He was there when I awoke this time. His hands still holding onto my bare back possessively as I drape over his chest. I rise up on my elbows and study his face. Dark stubble coats his jaw and upper lip. His eyelashes are so long they are brushing his cheek. Freckles dot his nose and cheekbones, almost the same color as his skin. I lean forward, the tip of my nose touching his.

One of his eyes opens and he stares at me. I smiled as wide as possible and squint my eyes.

"Wake up."

"What is it you want, little heathen?" he says softly before shifting his head back and forth so our noses rub; a weirdly intimate move.

"I want a pastry."

"A pastry?" I nod and smile.

"Mmhmm."

"And what kind of pastry does the princess want?" he asks his hand sliding up my back.

"One with chocolate," I respond before rolling over and pulling him with me. He leans over me.

"Anything for you," he whispers, his lips brushing mine before he jumps out of bed. His ass is smooth, round, but ten shades lighter than the rest of his body. I pull the blankets up to my neck and giggle as he slips on his trousers. "What is so funny?"

"You need to sunbathe without clothes."

"I'm not the only one with uneven skin," he retorts, and I feign shock. He shuts the door softly behind him, leaving me alone in the bed. I bite my lip as I remember the feel of him against me as I slept. His warmth, his touch, his—

"What the hell do you think you are doing?" Her voice snaps me out of my daze and my eyes widen.

"Mother!" I choke out as I sit up, keeping the blanket in front of me.

"I have never cared where you spent your evenings, but he isn't a whore, Moonlight. He will want something from you—from us," she yells, getting closer to the bed.

"Yes, he does. He wants me," I say with a lifted chin, but all that does it make her laugh.

"No, he wants your aether in his bloodline. He wants your *power*."

"You are the one who is trying to marry me off to common lords and humans!" I scream, almost forgetting to hold the blanket over my bare skin.

"So you want to marry him? Is that what you are suggesting?"

"No—"

"If you marry him—if you leave Zivell—I can't protect you, Moonlight. I can't keep you safe. I am trying to keep you safe."

"Sybil. My name is *Sybil*. I am more than just my aether. I am a person, mother. I am your daughter, and I don't need you to keep me safe!" I yell, anger boiling to the surface.

"You choose him, then? A man you barely know. A man who will take you to Noterra and *ruin* you."

"Why does there have to be a choice?"

"If you choose him, you'll *leave*."

"So what? It was bound to happen someday. You even wanted to send me to Dorin."

"To keep you safe!" she screams, her eyes flashing a fiery red before fading. "Moon—*Sybil*, think. Don't rush into this. I have no power out there. I cannot save you when everything blows up."

"I will save *myself*. I am stronger than you realize."

"You don't know what you are doing, and once you wed, you will be his property. Once you cross The Divide, I cannot keep you safe." She doesn't wait for a response. She just turns on her heel and walks out of the room, slamming the doors behind her.

"So they had a few with chocolate, so I brought them all..." His voice trails off as he takes me in. My knees are against my chest, my arms around them as I stare at the wall. "Little moon?" he asks as he sets down the platter and walks over.

"What is it you want me for?"

"What?"

"It can't be my charming personality; it can't be my face. Is it my aether? Are you only doing this because of my magic? Do you want me to breed you powerful little children until you get sick of me?" I drop my knees and look over at him.

"It's for all of it. For every part of you. You are frustrating and so damn beautiful. I can't stop thinking about you. I haven't since I was here a few months ago. All I can see is your face when I close my eyes."

"My mother thinks you just want my power," I whisper.

"That isn't it at all. If I wanted aether, I could choose any witch in your kingdom to take home, but I chose you."

"Why?"

"Because I am pulled to you. Like gravity. I have never wanted for anything until I met you." My eyes soften and I drop my legs, reaching for him.

"Take me home."

"Is that what you want? What you truly want? Things won't always be like this. It will be harder. I travel a lot, I work. I have duties."

"I will go where you go. I will travel where you travel. You said you wouldn't leave me again."

"Do you know what you are asking for? Being a princess here is relaxed, but in Noterra, there are rules you must uphold. You can't wander or explore alone. You can't dress like you do here. You'll be forced into gowns and taken to high teas and meals. You will be paraded about, and people will be scared of you."

"I don't care what other people think, Argent."

"Archie."

"*Prince.*" I smirk as I say it and he leans forward to grab my lip between his teeth. He rips at it, reopening the wound *again* and I wince.

"Three days at sea. That's how long it will take to get to Noterra," he says against my lips.

"Take me with you."

"No bathing chambers. Sea sickness," he adds.

"I think you forget who my father is," I say, licking the bead of blood off my lip.

"Is this what you want?"

"Yes."

"So be it," he responds, his lips falling into mine.

Chapter Twenty-Nine

The Moon

No goodbyes were had as I departed Zivell. I packed no bags; I packed no belongings. The only thing was my sirenstone, keeping me connected to my brother. We said our goodbyes and then went our separate ways. He decided to leave for Vodia earlier than before, leaving my mother alone.

But I think she prefers it that way.

Argent's arms are warm as they wrap around me. I watch the tropics fade as we get further and further out to sea. The green fading into a sea of blue and black as the light dimmed. He stayed with me through it all.

He stayed until I said it was okay to go.

Our chambers were anything but grand. A bed, writing desk, settee, and fireplace. The room was already warm, so no fire was lit, but I curled up on the bed and stared out the small porthole window on the wall, my hand resting on the pendant. I can still feel the connection to my brother, but it's dim—barely there, and it feels like an empty pit has formed in my heart.

Argent had matters to attend to, so he left me to do what I pleased. Though all it did was leave me feeling alone.

Did I make the wrong choice?

No. I didn't. Because in Noterra, I'll have Argent and I'll have Amaya. I won't be alone.

It was well into the night before he returned to the room, curling up around me, smelling of salt and sea.

"We will cross The Divide tomorrow afternoon."

"I've never crossed it," I whisper into the darkness. "Will it hurt?"

"No. You'll feel some pressure, and that never really goes away, but you get used to it." He speaks as if he knows, but I don't ask. His fingers trail up and down my arm, his lips pressing into my throat.

"What will it be like in Noterra?" I ask, breaking the silence. "Will they force me into other chambers?"

"You'll have a room of your own to retire to whenever you please, but you can stay with me as much as you'd like."

"Will they expect an engagement?" He exhales and kisses my throat again.

"Yes, but we will let my uncle worry about that. Engagements can last years, little moon. No need to buy a dress quite yet." I nod and close my eyes, pressing my backside harder against him. "Insatiable?"

"*Starving,*" I whisper back.

Morning brought cooked fish and stale bread, no pastries in sight. Argent tried to scrounge some up, but to no avail. He did find jam for the bread, which made it a little more palatable.

"Why doesn't Noterra have a better ship? This seems a little run-down for what I would expect the richest nation to possess."

"This isn't a Noterran ship. We bought our charter. If it were a Noterran ship you'd have ladies' maids and five course meals."

"Ladies' maids?"

"Women who attend to you." I stare at him. "Did you not have them in Zivell?"

"I am quite capable of dressing myself," I pout.

"In Noterra you'll have a handful of women whose job it is to serve you."

"I'd rather not."

"It will be expected of you." His voice hardens slightly, as if he's preparing for a fight.

"If you wanted a woman who did what was expected, you would have chosen one of the boring hags you claimed to know."

"Those boring hags are inconsequential in comparison to you."

"Damn straight." I smile, sipping the nasty water we were provided. "Do they know who you are?"

"Not at all." He laughs, biting into his crusty bread.

The sun was high in the sky when I felt it. It was a weird pressure and a pop and then...numbness. I could still feel the moonlight under my skin, but it was muffled. As if someone laid a blanket over it.

"Will I be able to use it at all?" I ask Argent as he leans over the side of the boat, stifling his own groan as we pass through.

"Yes, you will. It just won't be as strong."

"Will I be allowed to come back to visit?"

"Everywhere I go, remember?" He throws my braid over my shoulder before brushing his thumb along my bottom lip.

"Everywhere you go," I repeat. He kisses me softly before his eyes widen. "What is it?" I ask. He grabs my braid and brings it back over my shoulder. I glance down at the once silver strands, glossy black staring back.

"Your hair," he whispers. My hand reaches up and brushes the pendant, but I feel nothing. I feel numb. No connection. Any tether to my brother I had, has been broken.

A single tear escapes my eye, and I lean into Argent's chest, letting his warm arms soothe the sadness filling me.

Part Two: Noterra

CELAENA CUICO

Chapter Thirty

The Moon

"Princess, I don't know how things were on your...*land*, but here you must abide by our rules." Her stern voice causes an involuntary eye roll, which results in an equally stern look. Her graying hair and wrinkled skin do little to make her pretty when a scowl is permanently etched to her face.

"Well, Pheobe, my land was quite free and fun. I am not interested in being shoved in tight dresses that don't allow for movement. What if I have to fight? Protect myself?" I snap back as I prop my head on my hands. I've been laying on my stomach in a lace nightdress, my legs swinging behind me as I stare at the governess commanding my attention.

"You won't have a need to fight or protect yourself at high teas and luncheons," she retorts.

"I have no desire to partake in high teas and luncheons," I say with just as much disdain.

"Sybil, you have been here for nearly six months and have not even tried to integrate into our society. How do you expect to be queen someday if you don't represent

"Princess," I correct. "And I have no desire to be queen," I mutter as I realize how long I've been here. My birthday has come and passed, and now I have another eight months until I am twenty. Time is moving at an imperceivable rate.

"You are engaged to our heir, are you not?" I lift my hand and feign surprise as I stare at my naked finger.

"I do not see a ring on this finger. Do you? If you do, Pheebs, I fear I must consult a master for the sickness in your mind," I jest and can nearly see the steam shooting out of her ears.

"You are a petulant child, and I am done trying to help you." She storms out of the room, and I just laugh as I roll onto my back. It doesn't take long until a hand slides down my chest, to my stomach.

"You are only supposed to be a heathen in my presence, little moon. Phoebe is out there yelling about you being an absolute terror." His voice is sultry and soft as he nuzzles my neck. I inhale and tilt my head to allow him more access.

"Why must I have a governess? I am not in need of teaching, as if I am no more than a child." His free hand slowly wraps around my throat and yanks, forcing my eyes to his.

"My uncle likes you. He thinks you are amusing, but if you wish for an engagement, you must prove you can do this."

"Who says I want marriage?" I quirk and eyebrow and his own eyes heat.

"Sy—"

"Argent."

"*Archie*," he corrects.

"Please let me see your birth announcement that says Archie on it," I tease. His brows furrow and I lift my head to kiss his nose. "Why are you not at the council meeting?" I ask, changing the subject. He sighs and releases me, walking over to the settee and plopping down.

"I am to join my uncle on a trip to the Rosenthal Estate." I roll off the bed, my eyes wide as I plop down onto his lap.

"Please take me with you. You promised that we stay together," I beg, squeezing his cheeks in my hand.

"That is why I am here. You have twenty minutes before we depart." My lips slam into his before I scramble off his lap. His fingers grip my wrist, pulling me back. "*But* you must wear one of your gowns. Lord Rosenthal is not a kind man, and his son even less so."

"Is Evreux not your friend?"

"He is, but he is also someone who seeks to take everything that he finds pretty, that will include you."

"He cannot have what someone else has claimed." I smirk and stand.

"Mine," he says sternly before releasing me and standing as well. "I will be back shortly." On his way out, he pulls the rope on the wall to tell my ladies I am in need of assistance.

Thirty minutes later I am stepping into the courtyard, barely breathing. The corset is tightened against my ribs, threatening to snap them if I move in any way.

"Being late makes me look incapable, princess," Pheobe mutters next to me.

"I am not in the business of making you look capable, Pheobe," I mutter back.

"And what are you in the business of doing?" she spits, lightly gripping my elbow.

I smile at her, letting the small amount of moonlight I have access to, shine in my irises. "Being happy."

Chapter Thirty-One

The Moon

The royal carriage is grand. Large enough to seat the king, Argent and I with plenty of room to spare. King Jahara is a quiet and pensive man, but his focused gaze on my mouth is enough to give me goosebumps.

"Are you unable to breathe?" he says after twenty minutes of silence.

"Your Grace?"

"Your breathing is coming in quick pants as if you are unable to take in enough air. Are you alright?" Argent looks between us, and I bite my lip.

"It's the corset, Your Grace. I am afraid I am not used to the pressure."

"Wretched things," he scoffs. "Why are you wearing it then?"

"It is what's proper," I say softly, knotting my hands in my lap.

"According to who? Have you not been traipsing around my palace in loose dresses that usually are seen on those in bed?" He smirks and I find myself relaxing.

"I have, Your Grace."

"My nephew is hellbent on turning you into a proper Noterran woman, but I assure you, it is not necessary." I look at Argent and he furrows his brows.

"Uncle, I just wanted to ensure you accepted her."

"She has money, does she not? A respectable title that is technically above yours if we were to compare lands and blood. She is beautiful and well-spoken. Her mother has given her approval. What about her would I not approve of? Are you an exhibitionist, princess? Do you jump from bed to bed of the different noble men? Do I have to worry you'll aim for me next?" He started off teasing, but his tone became that of anger.

"N-no, Your Grace," I stammer.

"Archie, you are spending too much time with the Rosenthal boy and his friend. The Pinewell. Their outlook on a black and white world will doom us. Let the girl be who she is. Who are you to stifle her?" he lectures, and I bite my lip to keep from smiling.

"Of course, Uncle." Argent looks over at me and I suppress a giggle. "Would you like me to loosen your corset?" he asks.

"No, prince. I think I am fine until our journey home," I reply and squeeze his hand.

"Do you intend to sleep in that corset? Because we will be staying a few days." I glare at him and the king snorts.

The ride to the Rosenthal Estate was anything but quick as their grand home is located on the other side of Port Aston, the largest port on the entire continent.

Their home is covered in vines and roses, the country's flower. Suited men and gowned women line the entry way in a half-inviting, half-terrifying manner. I reach for Argent's hand, but he shakes his head slightly.

Not being married essentially means we must be supervised at all times, although that is not the case when we are at the palace. I sigh and clamp my hands together in front of my waist, slightly bending my elbows.

A tall, stately looking man walks out of the entryway door. His tunic and trousers are perfectly tailored and stark red, matching the roses growing along the stone walls. He approaches us with ease, a smile across his face. He doesn't bow, like I expected, but instead, pulls King Jahara into a hug.

"Jahara, you are looking older," he jokes as he pats his back.

"You have at least eight years on me, Henry," King Jahara snorts back, returning the hug. Lord Henry looks at Argent and pats his shoulder before taking a step to his right and letting his eyes fall upon me. His eyes widen in surprise, his mouth gaping open slightly. He recovers quickly.

"And who might this be?" He raises his hand in invitation, and I slowly set mine in it. He lifts it to his lips and kisses the back of it.

"This is Princess Sybil Monvoison of Zivell," The king says.

"It is a pleasure to make your acquaintance, my lord." I smile, but I don't bow. It would be below my station.

"I was unaware a princess was of age when the queen and I arranged for the Lady Amaya to join our family." I slip my hand out of his rather roughly, returning it to its place.

"I wasn't for sale." I smile and tilt my head. His eyes flinch, his pupils darkening. But it's not fear or power, it's amusement I see.

"Well, I believe the cooks have prepared a feast for your arrival." He claps his hands before spinning on his heel and leading us inside.

"Sorry." I mouth as I look at Argent. He smirks, his dimples showing. His hand brushes my back, urging me forward.

The grand table is set for thirty with only four present. Lord Henry sits at the head of the table, his face full of irritation as we stare at empty plates.

"I apologize, Jahara. My son and his wife should have been present by now." As he speaks, the doors to the dining hall open and in walks a young man that looks like an exact replica of Henry. Blonde hair, blue eyes, angry brows, and a clenched jaw. He weirdly reminds me of the man in my vision, as if they could be related.

It's the woman behind him that makes me jump from my chair, despite what is proper.

Her golden hair and gray eyes are shining, as if she has been flourishing in Noterra. A small boy is gripping her hand while her other is resting on a slightly swollen belly.

"Ami!" I yell as I rush her. My arms go around her neck, and she throws hers around me.

"Sy?" she questions, as she pulls back. Her eyes are pooled with tears, her nose instantly running. "What are you doing here?" she demands.

"I moved to the palace a few months ago." Her face falls slightly as she looks behind me. I glance down at the small boy clutching his mother's hands. "Hello there. My name is Sybil." I hold out my hand and he takes it gently, the child less than a year and a half.

"This is Tobias, Sy."

"Well, Tobias. You are just as cute as a little monkey." I poke his nose and he smiles. His golden-copper curls fall into his face, blocking his bright blue eyes that remind me of ice. My smile falters and I quickly force it to return. I stand and take her hand. "Another?" I ask as I glance at her stomach. She nods.

"About six months along, I believe." She smiles and rubs her stomach. It is only then that I see her husband staring at me.

"Hello, Lord Evreux." I smile and hold out a hand. His eyes are fixed on mine, a look of wonder about them.

"I take it you are Sybil?" he asks, gripping my hand tightly and pulling me slightly towards him.

"Princess Sybil Monvoison of Zivell," Argent says sternly, coming up next to me and pulling Evreux into a hug. "Good to see you, brother," he says, but Evreux's eyes never leave mine.

I glance nervously at Amaya, who is staring at her husband with confusion. But her look quickly fades to anger as she follows his line of sight.

"The food grows cold, and my patience runs thin. *Sit,*" Lord Henry snaps and we all hurry to our seats.

Chapter Thirty-Two

The Moon

Argent stays close to my side, putting Amaya directly in front of me. A nursemaid came to retrieve Tobias after we all sat, and I found myself saddened. I wanted to spend time with the little boy.

Ami on the other hand, was full of chatter. Detailing her life in Noterra and how the Rosenthal's have been more than welcoming. But it was the mention of how busy it had been at the estate the last few months that had me questioning their motives.

She started to mention the casual stream of men who are in the royal military that have come and gone and stayed at the estate. But it was Lord Henry who cut her off to discuss other matters. Her face had dropped and even Argent looked skeptical as the subject was changed.

"So, Jahara, tell me what has been going on in the palace as of late? It has been quite some time since I have made the journey." Lord Henry's voice is cool and calculated and I find myself eating my roast chicken in silence.

"Nothing of consequence, Henry. Just making sure our country stays running. What of you? I see the men Maeryn has traded for Amaya have not yet made their way across the sea?" My chewing slows and we all turn towards Henry. By all, I mean Argent and I. Amaya didn't seem phased and Evreux seemed...like he was angry. As if he was unhappy with the direction the conversation was going.

"Oh, just haven't had time to organize their travels to Zivell," he responds with ice in his tone. Henry turns to Evreux and smiles. "I think your son is due to be put to bed if your wife would be so inclined to care for my grandson." Amaya only nods and rises, exiting the room quickly before I could even say anything. As if being ordered about was a normal occurrence.

"Yes, I do think it is quite late. Maybe all of the children should retire?" King Jahara supplies, his lips pressed into a thin line.

"As you wish, Uncle, but I haven't been a child for some time," Argent snorts, rising from his seat and helping me up.

"The maids can show you two to your *separate* chambers," Henry quips and I don't turn around.

"Goodnight, Your Grace." I bow slightly to Jahara, and he offers me a tender smile.

With my hand resting on Argent's arm, we quickly exit the dining hall. Evreux's feet are silent, and I don't know he's behind us until I feel a sharp tug on Argent's shoulder.

"What say you and I head to town? There is a lovely new brothel I have been frequenting." His arm wraps around Argent's neck as he tries to entice him.

"It has been a long journey, Ev. I think I should bathe and sleep."

"Come on, Viktor should be there," the lord's son whines as if it's something that usually gives him his way.

"What is he doing out of Chatis?"

"Visiting."

"If you two will excuse me, I must retire to my room." I smile and spin on my heel.

"You could come with us. I think the men of Noterra would enjoy you,

I know I wou—" A hand grazes my elbow, and I flinch.

"Enough! Come on, little moon," Argent snaps before brushing my lower back and guiding me to the stairs and away from Evreux.

"Gods, how is he your friend?" I snort under my breath as we ascend.

Not much time later, I am slipping out my chamber door in nothing but a nightgown. I quickly glance up and down the hallway before racing down a few doors and slipping inside another room.

Arms wrap around me from behind and I squeal, only for his hand to cover my mouth.

"Took you long enough," he snarls, biting my earlobe as he spins me around, my legs flying through the air. I grip onto his arm as he sets me down and tightens his grip around me. "I am sorry for Evreux's behavior."

"The actions of another are not your fault, Argent."

"Archie," he corrects.

"Argent," I respond.

"Why must you refuse me?"

"Why must you have a nickname that doesn't work with your given name?" I snort and pinch his forearm. "Did you already bathe?"

"Yes."

"Did you brush your teeth?"

"Yes."

"Did you—"

"The only thing I have left to do, you tiresome little heathen, is bed *you*."

"I think I would like to go to bed, I am rather tired—" My voice turns into a giggle as his lips slam into mine. His fingers dig into my hips, no doubt causing bruises. As he guides me to the bed, lifting me up onto the mattress, my eyes flutter open, and I swear I see a pair of blue eyes in the wall staring back at me.

Chapter Thirty-Three

The Moon

"Who are you?" I spin on my heel as the sound of a gruff, male voice flits across the room. The orange juice in my hand spills over the edge, landing on the stone floor.

"Damnit!" I mutter as I quickly bend down to wipe it with the hem of my dress. When I look up, the man is still there. He's young, probably the same age as Argent. His hair is short and a muted chestnut brown, matching his eyes. His face is pale, as if he doesn't see much sun. A green tunic and black trousers are all that covers him, besides a small sheen of sweat.

"I asked you a question," he says, and I raise my brows.

"Excuse me?"

"Who are you?" he repeats.

"Someone who is well above your station and could get you beheaded."

"Do you not know who I am?" he presses.

"Obviously not," I snort, setting the orange juice down next to a heaping plate of pastries I want to dig in to.

"Lord Viktor Pinewell of Chatis. One of the most noble families in the north," he says diplomatically, as if I care.

"Ah. Makes sense. Except, your father is the lord, and you, are just Mr. Pinewell." I clasp my hands together and walk slowly towards him. "And I am Princess Sybil Monvoison of Zivell." He balks, his eyes darkening in either anger or lust, I can't tell. I tilt my chin. "I'm waiting." He quickly drops to a bow, his knee pressing into the stone floor.

"I see you two have met!" Evreux rounds the corner, patting his friend on the shoulder. "She's something, isn't she?" Viktor stands and smirks, an evil gleam in his eyes.

"That she is."

"Where did Argent go?" I ask, returning to my juice.

"Archie? He said he would meet us down here," Evreux says uninterested as he follows me to the table. I take a sip of my juice and turn towards them. Evreux's brows furrow as he reaches forward and brushes the corner of my lip. I flinch and step back. "You had some juice—" He says with a smile before grabbing his own glass.

"Tell me, Ev. How did you get so lucky to have two beautiful women living in your estate?" Viktor jokes as he steps between us. I take another cautious step back, feigning interest in a piece of art on the wall.

"Well Amaya is a foreigner, and so is our lovely princess."

"Except I don't live here," I say with a voice laced with irritation.

"Where do you live, Sybil?" Viktor asks and I turn to face them.

"At the palace." His eyes widen in surprise.

"Are you engaged to Archie?" he asks.

"No," I supply. Evreux's eyes narrow and the color sends a shiver down my spine. Was he watching us last night?

"Sybil is a free woman," Evreux jokes stepping towards me. I sidestep away from his all-too-friendly hand and return my juice to the banquet table.

"Where is your wife?" I ask him, resting my hands in front of me. "I think I would like to spend time with my oldest friend."

"I sent her home," he says with a shrug.

"Do you both not live here?"

"No. Our main residence is elsewhere. We won't reside in the estate until my father passes." He steps closer and I find my pulse quickening.

"Well, then I must find Argent."

"He will be joining us."

"Is there a reason you do not want me to leave this room, my lord?" I press. "You both have forgone formality in referring to me with a proper title. You have touched me without permission, and now you are lying to me. What do you think will happen if—"

"Nothing will happen. You have no power here. You are not *our* princess. On this land you are nothing. You are in my home and if I want—" He stops as he looks behind me.

"If you want *what*?" Argent says behind me, and my shoulders relax.

"Nothing," Viktor says as he slaps his friend on the shoulder. "He meant nothing by it. We had a long night and I think our friend here needs to eat something." Argent's hand brushes my elbow and I step back into him.

"I think I will take the princess on a tour of your gardens," he says and the lords just nod. He pulls me away and when we get to the hallway he spins me around. "What happened?"

"I would like to go home," I whisper, glancing behind him. His fingers tighten.

"Zivell?" he says softly, fear lacing his voice.

"No, the palace," I correct, and he relaxes. He pulls me into his chest, and I tighten my arms around him.

"We can leave tomorrow. I promise."

"No. Today. I feel like something is off," I whisper.

"Little moon," he chastises.

"You know I have sight. I have intuition too. Trust me. I don't feel safe here."

"Come with me." He says after a few seconds, pulling me down the hall.

"Where are we going?"

"Somewhere private."

Chapter Thirty-Four

His hand stays firmly planted in mine as he drags me through a garden of roses. The air is crisper down here, colder than it is at the palace. My feet move quickly so I can keep up with him. He's silent as we weave though what I am realizing is a maze, before we reach the center.

A beautiful fountain spirting water lies in the middle. Roses form the body of a woman with wings, as if it's created by faeries chiseled out of stone. The statue sits in the center of the fountain, the sunlight turning her marble skin a pale yellow.

"It's beautiful," I whisper as I stare up at it. He spins around and grabs my face.

"Marry me." My eyes widen.

"What?"

"Marry me. We are already engaged."

"No, we aren't," I cut him off.

"The second I agreed to bring you with me was us being engaged. You know that." I bite my lip as I stare into his emerald eyes. "We are engaged. We have been for eight months. Marry me, little moon. Be mine so I can protect you." I rip my face out of his hands.

"That's the only reason?" I spit.

"No. Marry me because I am in love you. I have loved you since you found me at the tree. I have loved you since I claimed you as mine over a year ago. We have been skirting around and pretending we don't feel something for fifteen months. You are nineteen, you will be twenty in five months. You are here. You've been here for a long time. I am turning twenty-two in a few weeks. What are we waiting for?"

"This isn't exactly a romantic proposal," I snort.

"I love you."

"And I you."

"Say it."

"I love you, Argent," I say softly.

"Archie," he corrects.

"I love you. Every part of you."

"Then marry me."

"No."

"Why?"

"Because you haven't been honest with me." He steps back, shock evident on his face.

"What?"

"What magic do you possess?" I ask, crossing my arms.

"Excuse me?" His eyes widen and I know he's avoiding the question. Avoiding the truth. But why? Is it fear?

"What magic do you possess? Because you flinched and groaned when we crossed The Divide months ago. And you disappear. Sometimes when you are angry or tired, you leave the palace and don't return for some time. You smell constantly of animals and nature. You are keeping something important from me."

"You have been waiting this long to ask me?" he asks bewildered.

"I want you to offer the information, Argent. I didn't want to pry it from you."

"I have none."

"You are *lying*. I saw a spotted tail. Some sort of feline. The only felines we have in our forests are panthers. Nothing spotted. What *are* you? And why are you lying to me? To *me*?" I step forward staring up into his eyes.

"Ailuranthrope," he blurts out.

"What?" I stutter. Is that a different language?

"I'm a feline shifter. I have one other form. Like the wyvos, but my forms are jaguar and human."

"Argent..." I whisper, stepping away. I knew; I knew deep down, but still. "How? Is Jahara?" I ask.

"No. It came from my mother. She was a shifter from Tatus my father fell in love with. As a second son, he could choose his mate. And he chose her. But they both died after I was born."

"So this means..."

"What?"

"It means that if we have children, Argent, they will be full blood."

"Yes," he says, knowing the direction I am headed.

"Do you know what kind of power someone could possess with a full-blooded child in their control?" My voice raises and I clench my fists. Is this what he always wanted? Is this why he wanted me?

"I wouldn't use any of my children."

"Not you, Argent. Your uncle. The council. It's dangerous."

"No. It's advantageous. We would rule the continent. Our children would rule the continent as our heirs. High King or High Queen. I have always wanted a daughter."

"Did you plan this?" His face falls and I step back. "You planned this. When you came to Zivell you already had this plan in mind!"

"Yes. When I said I was in Zivell for my uncle, I wasn't lying. I was there to get you."

"I cannot believe this," I whisper, my throat tight. "You lied to me. You schemed to marry me. To have my children. You wanted powerful children. He wanted powerful children." Tears line my eyes.

"Yes."

"Why didn't you tell me?" I scream again. Smacking my hands across his chest. He flinches and catches my elbows. "I still would have said yes."

"What?"

"I didn't want to marry Bastian. I didn't want to stay in Zivell or go to Dorin. All my thoughts were of you. You didn't have to lie. I still would have left with you, you stupid *imbecile*!"

"Sybil." His voice catches, unshed tears pooling in his eyes.

"Archie."

"You called me Archie."

"I don't know what to do. This is a lot of information."

"Marry me. People don't have to know about our children. If we even have children. Be my wife. Be my other half." He steps forward, holding me against him. "I love you. And while getting married is my uncle's wish, it is also mine. Not for your magic. But for you. I have never wanted anyone or anything until I met you."

"You already used that line."

"Doesn't make it less true." I bite my lip and grip his tunic.

"Okay."

"Okay?" I nod hesitantly.

"I'll marry you."

Chapter Thirty-Five

The Moon

We made love in the garden maze. I think it was the first time we truly did it out of love. While I have loved him for a long time, our need for each other was always carnal, but this wasn't.

This was like needing to breathe.

He retied my corset loosely, allowing me to easily breathe, before he pressed his lips to my neck.

"A daughter?" I smile, bringing up his revelation from earlier.

"Yes."

"If you had a daughter, what would you want to name her?" I ask with a smirk.

"My mother's name was Elaenor," he says softly.

"It's a beautiful name." I turn in his arms. "I would like a daughter someday too." I rest into him, and he kisses the top of my head.

"We can go home."

"Promise?"

"Yes. We can leave tonight."

"Thank you." I turn in his arms again and press my lips to his. "You better get me a ring." I smirk.

Chapter Thirty-Six

The Moon

Jahara stayed, and we returned to the palace. The ride was long, but we were anything but bored in the royal carriage by ourselves. And when we finally made it back, we stayed in Archie's room until Jahara returned. Only when he was announced did we decide to finally rise out of bed.

"Do we have to?" I pout.

"Yes. We must see what he and Henry spoke about," I whine and roll onto my back, stretching. Archie leans forward, pressing his lips to my stomach. "I am hopeful there is a little heir in there."

"That would be too soon. We aren't even wed."

"I don't care. I just want her to come out looking like you." He smirks and pulls my hand. "Come on," I groan and slide off the mattress before grabbing the linen dress off the settee.

"At least I don't have to wear a corset anymore," I mutter as I step into the silk shoes I was given.

"Never again, although they are ravishing." He licks his lips and drags me to the door.

It bursts open, hitting Archie in the face. He falls back, taking me with him. I land on my hip and wince as I reach for him

"Archie!" I yell as he wipes blood off his face.

"Sy!" he screams as he looks behind me. Someone wraps their arms around my waist, ripping me off the floor. I slam my palms down on their flesh, sending moonlight into their skin. Whoever it is yells, their deep voice all too familiar.

I am thrown back to the ground and whoever it is grabs my ankle, dragging me towards them. I kick out, before rolling over to see Viktor standing there with burns on his arms.

Archie rises, pulling me to his side.

"What the fuck are you doing?" he yells, but that's all he is able to say before something hits him on the back of the head. He drops and I turn to see Evreux. As I expose my back to Viktor, his hand comes over my mouth, the sickly scent of something sweet permeating my nose before everything goes black.

Screaming. All I hear is screaming. It's coming from my mouth, but it's a mouth that isn't mine. I look up as blood pools over the marble floor, a head with dirty blonde hair rolling away from a slumped body.

Oh, Gods.

I look up at his golden hair, his icy eyes. He looks so familiar. He looks so much like—

"I knew you were doing something behind our back." His voice is rough, as if he's in pain. I blink away the impending headache, my head resting on the white marble. I glance up at King Jahara who is being pressed against the wall by Henry, a knife to his throat. I slowly sit up, looking around.

Archie is passed out to my left and I quickly crawl over to him, pulling his head into my lap. I tap his cheek while looking for anything to protect us.

"Archie, wake up," I whisper. I see nothing. It's just the four of us in the throne room. His eyes flutter open and I almost gasp in relief, but I don't have time. I need to do something. "I love you," I whisper as I slide his head off me and rise. His hand goes weakly around my ankle, but I shake it off.

I run over to Henry, putting my hands around his neck. The silvery shafts of light illuminate his veins as he drops his knife and falls to his knees with a yell. Jahara's eyes widen as he looks behind me. Viktor appears, his eyes filled with a wicked gleam.

"You are going to be fun to break." He slaps me and before I can fall to the ground, he grabs my shoulders. I reach up to grab his arm when I feel the prick of a needle. I gasp as ice spreads through my veins.

"What is this?" I whisper breathlessly, moonlight fading into nothing.

"Assurance that you won't be a threat," he growls before pressing his lips to mine. I weakly attempt to push him off, but prove unsuccessful.

"Get off of me!" I scream, my nails digging into his scalp. He's ripped away and Jahara is there, pulling me to my feet.

"Run, Sybil. This is a coup. *Run*," he commands me, and I glance behind him to Archie.

"I'm not leaving him."

"*Go!*" he yells pushing me towards the door.

"No!" I scream back and run to Archie. I slide on the ground and help him sit up. "We have to go. Get up." He nods, blood pouring out of a gash in his head.

"I'll slow you down," he whispers. I shake my head, urging him to his feet.

"I don't care." The tears come hot and wet down my cheeks as he gets to his feet. Jahara is there, the three of us standing to the side.

"I told you I couldn't protect you."

Chapter Thirty-Seven

The Moon

Her voice cuts through my panic as if it's as sharp as a blade. I spin on my heel to face my mother.

"*Mother*?" I whisper just as Jahara whispers, "*Maeryn*?"

"I told you, Moonlight. I warned you."

"Mother, what is happening?" I step towards her, but Jahara blocks me.

"This was what you sold Amaya for?" Jahara asks, and my mother just nods. Only then does Evreux walk in with her; with my best friend. A knife to her belly. My hand instinctively reaches for the pendant around my neck, but it's gone.

My mother has it in her hand.

"Don't do this," I beg, willing my voice to stay strong.

"Jahara is weak. His goals of unity and peace are those that belong to a child. Henry wants strength. *I* want strength. I want the continent—and Henry will get that for us. He will get it for you." I gasp as I stare at her.

"You were going to marry me off to Henry?" I yell stepping forward.

"You were going to stage a coup and then marry me off to him?" She doesn't respond and just glances over to where Henry is leaning against the wall, burns around his neck. "I will die first." I step back, Archie wrapping his arm around me, his legs unsteady.

"You no longer have a choice." It's quick, but the bolt of fire that flies through the air hits Jahara right in the forehead. His eyes widen in shock, as do mine, as I stare at the hole in his head. He drops quickly, smoke and blood pouring from his wound.

"I will kill her," Evreux says from the side, the knife still pressed to Amaya's belly. A stream of blood is pouring down her pale dress.

"What do you want!" Archie yells, his voice weak. I tighten my grip on him.

"I want the power." His head whips towards Viktor as he throws a blade into Henry's neck. Amaya screams and Archie and I jump back as Henry gasps for air. Blood pours down his neck as he slumps to the ground, confusion widening his eyes.

"You want to be king?" I ask.

"Take it! I don't want it!" Archie yells pulling us closer to the wall.

"Do you think anyone would accept me if you were still alive?" Evreux asks, directing the question to Archie. "Besides, I owe the Pinewell's a debt." He looks at me, and when I turn to face Viktor, he has the same wicked gleam in his eye.

"No. I won't do it. I will kill you."

"You think Viktor happened upon an essence that will render you human?" my mother asks as she shakes her head. "I gave it to him."

"This doesn't make any sense. How does this work? He's already married!"

"But Viktor is not. And his father is dead."

"So?"

"Jahara *was* High King, child. He ruled over the continent. With him gone, we can separate. We can be our own countries fully. We will have our own laws and government. We wouldn't answer to them. You will be Queen of Chatis."

"No."

"Yes."

"Archie," I whisper. He tightens his arms around me.

"This isn't happening."

"Can you shift?" I whisper, but I feel the shake of his head. Resolve settles over me as I stare at Amaya, Viktor, Evreux, and my mother. "Let her go."

"I will give you a choice, Sybil," Evreux says.

"Let. Her. Go," I repeat.

"Amaya or Archie. Pick."

"Leave her out of this, please. Just let her go," Archie says from behind. Then I see it.

I see what I saw in the bath.

And I know what's going to happen. He's going to stab Amaya's stomach and kill her unborn child.

"You can have me. Okay?" I say, raising my hands. "You can have me. Just let them go. Please," I beg.

"Stop it," Archie hisses. I spin in his arms.

"I love you," I whisper. I rise on my toes and kiss him before whispering in his ear. When I finish my confession, I stare at his eyes widened with fear.

"No." He shakes his head. "My moon." Tears drip from his eyes as he kisses my forehead.

"It's not about us anymore, Archie," I say with finality. When I pull out of his arms, I take a backwards step towards Viktor, before turning away. "Let them both go," I say glancing at my mother.

"No." Is all she says before his scream pierces the air. When I spin around to face Archie, there is a hole in his chest. I scream—a blood curdling scream— that tears through my body. Viktor's arms go around me, holding me back as

Archie holds my gaze.

He drops to his knees, his eyes never leaving mine as the blood wells up in his mouth before spilling over.

I scream over and over and over again, fighting against Viktor. Begging for my aether to come.

The one thing that would always protect me.

The one thing that had always been mine.

The one thing I would give up just to feel Archie's hands against my skin one more time.

But I can't.

Silence spreads throughout the throne room. The only noise is my failing voice as the scream tears through my throat. I taste the blood in my mouth, feel the pain in my knees as I drop to the marble. I try to reach for him, but I'm held back.

I hear sobs to my right and see Amaya's eyes wide and her hand covering her mouth. Evreux drops the knife and stares dumfounded at his body. As if he didn't expect for this to happen, even if it was his plan.

My mother sighs and drops her arm before turning towards me.

"I warned you, Moonlight."

A ringing starts in my ears. A ringing fueled by pain and by anger.

A feeling that I know will transfer.

Not to any one person.

Not to any one being.

But to a generation.

Revenge.

Revenge for her father.

Revenge for her mother.

Revenge for the life she will never have.

I know now who that girl was I kept seeing. The sadness in her eyes mirrors mine.

Mirrors her mother's.

Elaenor.

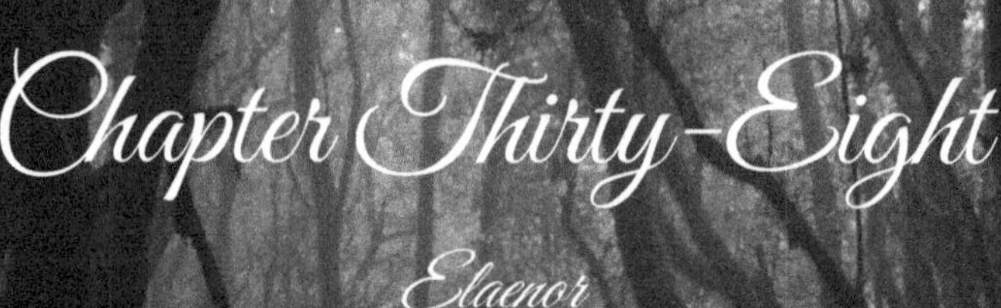

Everything plays through my mind like a book of memories. Memories that aren't mine. She was so young, my mother. My father, a face I had never seen before.

I want to scream; I want to cry. But nothing comes out.

My father was murdered. The man who raised me assaulted my mother and aided in the death of my father. My own grandmother, Maeryn, the still reigning queen of Zivell. She *killed* my father.

I heard my mother's soft voice whispering into Archie's ear.

"*I'm pregnant.*" Her breathy voice said, cracking. "*And I will protect her, I promise.*"

It was me. And Enzo. We were in her stomach. And we were there when my father was murdered.

My eyes are closed but I feel the wind whipping past me, drying my tears before they have a chance to fall. And then I hit it. Soft grass caresses my back, and I open my eyes.

But it's not grass along my back. It's a cushion.

When my eyes open, all I see is darkness. What happened to the wind and grass?

I'm in a carriage.

I reach for the window and slide the curtain back. Endless trees and a starry night sky greet me. I look down at the gravel and push the door open, stepping out into the night.

I glance to my left and see two horses, standing still in front of the carriage. No rider in sight.

No.

A shout causes me to jump, and I run towards the front of the two beasts. A dark lump on the ground causes my heart to race. This *can't* be happening. I run forward, dropping to my knees as Erik slowly bleeds to death, a dagger protruding out of his chest.

"Run." He croaks.

"No, no, no." I push on his wound, trying to stave off the bleeding. "This isn't real." Snapping branches causes me to flinch, as I see him step out of the tree line.

Jeremiah. Alive.

"This can't be real." I whisper as my eyes freeze on his body, stalking towards me.

"Elaenor, run!" Erik chokes out. I scramble to my feet and break out into a run, crossing the tree line. I push as fast as I can, ignoring the rocks and branches as they slice through my feet.

This can't be real.

This can't be happening.

A warm hand grabs the back of my neck and slams me to the ground. A body climbs atop me, dark eyes staring into my soul.

My life. The entire life I lived. The deaths that occurred. The people I've loved. It's all gone. It's all gone, and I am back here.

Where it all began.

A dagger slams into my thigh as I stare up at him. I don't flinch. I don't scream. I've been through worse.

This is a chance. A chance to do better. A chance to do more.

My hand goes into my pocket, and I slide the glass arrowhead out. The sirenstone from my brother. The brother who is out there, waiting for me.

"I've never had a princess befo–" I swing my arm and slam the sharpened point into his temple, cutting him off. His body drops to the ground beside me, and I stare at the gaping hole in the side of his head. Rustling behind me causing me to spin around, still on my knees.

It's Aleksander, or his friends. I'm ready for them this time. My arm is raised, poised to strike, but the man who steps through the trees isn't who I thought.

Golden blonde hair with half of it tied back. Blue eyes sparkling in what little moonlight there is. His sword is out, ready to fight. His eyes find mine and a choked sob escapes my lips. He sees me there, dagger still in the air and he smirks. He sheaths his sword and crouches down next to me.

"Well, it looks like you didn't need my help here." He cocks his head to the side, his eyes searching mine, before he extends a hand to help me up. "Hi, my name is Theo. And you are?"

ABOUT THE AUTHOR

Celaena Cuico *(sell-ay-nuh coo-we-co)* was born and raised in Southern California. Celaena endured hardships such as an abusive significant other and the unknown that comes with moving across the country twice for a job. She is the author of The Diadem, a series about a young girl thrown into a life of jumping from kingdom to kingdom to survive, and The Soulless, a series about the God of the Underworld's minions and their lives forced to collect souls for him.

NOTE FROM THE AUTHOR

To my best friends: Jac, Vee, Haydn, Annie, and Ris, you guys are my rocks, my biggest supporters and the ones I would never want to do any of this authoring crap without. I love you all so so so MUCH!

To my sister, Myrissa, thank you for being my sounding board, my therapist, and my home all in one.

To my professional handlers, Erin and Heather, my life would be chaos without you. Your support, your help, your wrangling of my undiagnosed ADHD are the only reason anything gets done. Your trauma mommy loves you!

To the girl who constantly brings Elaenor, and soon Sybil, to life – Beth. You angel. You perfect human. Thank you for being my Elaenor.

To my dear friends – Sara, Meghan (Fireheart), Thea Green, Thea Guanzon, AND SO MANY MORE – I am so grateful to have you in my corner. You all provide so much happiness to my life, and without you, I wouldn't be here.

And to my fiancé, Maggie, thank you for allowing me the time and the space to develop my creativity. Knowing you are able to keep the house, and psycho dogs, under control so that I can live out my dreams, is something I could never repay. I love you. Endlessly.

Forever yours,

XO Cel